Strained Relations

ALISON CAIRNS

Strained Relations

St. Martin's Press
New York

Library of Congress Cataloging in Publication Data

Cairns, Alison.
  Strained relations.

  I. Title.
PR6053.A373S8   1984   823'.914   83-11155
ISBN 0-312-76382-4

First published in Great Britain in 1983 by
William Collins Sons & Co. Ltd

First U.S. Edition

10 9 8 7 6 5 4 3 2 1

CONTENTS

CHAPTER 1. THURSDAY

The afternoon of Thursday July 16 was one of intense humidity and heat. As temperatures soared all over the country, Londoners stripped and showered under the fountains in Trafalgar Square. On motorways overheated vehicles were pulled over on to the hard shoulder, their drivers sweating and swearing in impotent frustration.

Around the ragged coastline of the West Country the seas lay becalmed, benign and blue; and tourists in their thousands rushed like lemmings to every cove and creek: to crush and crowd, to splash and squeal and swim, in joyful celebration.

In the village churchyard on a slope above Treskellan the flowers on a yet unsettled grave wilted and dropped in a dying flame of scarlet and gold: the grave of Sebastian Quinn, beloved doctor, *bon vivant*, and father of Russell, of Christopher and of Alexis.

Christopher Quinn was teaching history at the seat of learning administered by the Inner London Education Authority known as the James Barncroft Comprehensive School; this out of respect for a local councillor prematurely dead through excess of devotion to the demands of local government. The school had been built in the late 'sixties, a glass and concrete affirmation of the belief that in education could be found the antidote to most of the evils of deprivation found in a district well on the road to inner city decay.

A worthy, if mistaken, belief.

The catchment area which fed its young to Barncroft Comprehensive embarked on a peaceful policy of noncooperation with all attempts to have its aspirations moved upmarket. In time the buildings became decently vandalized. One by one the members of the staff with special responsibility for pastoral care packed up their files and left. Those who remained grew weekly more proficient in the writing of reports for the attention of the Juvenile Courts.

Within the school, youthful initiative expressed itself in a proliferation of free enterprise subcultures, small and beautiful and mostly anti-social. The Headmaster lost little time in incorporating into his personal philosophy the concept of flexibility. This led on naturally to the acceptance of persistent truancy and a general amnesty for those who were none too keen on the idea of homework. It became his primary concern, he was fond of telling staff meetings, to ensure that Barncroft Comprehensive was known above all as a *happy* school. Or, as Hugh Purcell with his doctorate in maths was equally fond of saying, if you can't take a joke you shouldn't have joined.

When the school bell released Christopher's thirty unstreamed fourth-formers from a double period on the Peasants' Revolt, they left the room with all the decorum of a cavalry charge. He knew he should have intervened, called them back and insisted on a delayed and orderly exit. But today his sympathies were with the youngsters. The heat was overpowering; compounded with the smell of dust and chalk and fit young bodies, it had left the room rank and fetid with stale air. A waste of everybody's time and effort to have stopped the flight. It was easy to rationalize, so close to the end of term.

Thanks be to God.

He crossed from his desk to the classroom windows. Three enormous sheets of plate glass had been designed by someone wise in the ways of children. They provided gaps for ventilation so shallow as to discourage all attempts to propel any of their number out on to the concrete paving thirty feet below.

Chris crouched low to breathe in great gulps of air, warm but fresh; pressed his aching forehead against the hard hot glass; watched with relief the departing hordes push and jostle and fight their way to freedom.

He had rarely felt as drained as he was now: tired beyond belief.

'Sir?'

A voice behind him: young, female, respectful. He turned with a scowl of irritation which lifted as he recognized the girl.

'Yes, Maria. What can I do for you?'

Half an hour later he gathered up the exercise books he must mark that night, walked along the echoing corridor to the stairs; left by the main entrance and crossed the playground, spattered white with chewing gum trampled underfoot. His grey Volkswagen was one of only two left in the car park. It must be later than he'd thought.

Within ten minutes he was pulling up at the kerb outside his home. Chandlers Grove was a wide tree-lined road of identical houses built between the wars. Each house contained four two-bedroomed self-contained flats, two on the first floor, two at ground level. A pleasant district, the estate agents claimed with unusual accuracy. Chandlers Grove was indeed a pleasant road, of pleasant people living in pleasant homes.

There was not much else one could say about it.

The front of the house was lying in shadow, the doors and windows open to allow what breeze there was to flow through its rooms. Exercise books under one arm, Chris locked the car door and crossed the garden, a rectangle of well-watered green bordered by antirrhinums, yellow and bronze; up two steps to the hall, oatmeal carpeted, wide enough only for a small Adam table reflecting in its depths a cream telephone, a single-stemmed rose in a slender crystal glass.

He could hear Caroline preparing drinks in the kitchen, called out that he was home, and turned right into the sitting-room, shaded and cool. He heaved the exercise books into a chair, pitched his car keys after them and sank into the cream velvet depths of the sofa; locked his hands behind his head and tried to ease the tension from neck and shoulders.

Caroline, trim and fresh, pushed the door wide with her elbow: crisp lemon top and tailored slacks of chocolate brown. In silence she handed him a tall glass of frosted lemonade.

'You're late.'

She retreated to the doorway, her own glass in one hand. The throbbing ache which had been gnawing away behind his right eye for most of the afternoon hardened into a jab of pain. Not now, please God. Not now.

After seven years of marriage Chris still believed that Caroline was the most exciting woman he'd ever met; her attraction lying not so much in any conventional beauty — still less in being pretty — but in the animation and vitality which characterized everything about her. Even now Caroline seemed incapable of doing anything by halves; she was warm and generous, vivacious and enthusiastic, passionate in both her loves and hatreds.

There were those who disliked her alarming honesty, her directness of manner, her contempt for the pretentious and the phoney. She had little time for the loser, the whiner, the incompetent; but for those in genuine trouble or despair she had immense reserves of loyalty and strength.

It was not until after they were married that Chris was to discover that Caroline suffered from a compulsive need for the occasional blazing row in the way that other addicts require their chosen brand of fix: at fairly predictable intervals. The eruption would be sudden,

fiercely dramatic and stage-managed to perfection: hazel
eyes alight with outrage, chestnut curls tossing in defiance,
extravagant gestures wild but graceful. Everything Caroline
did was touched with grace. It was the only trait of Caroline's which had ever disturbed him. But it did. Always.
'I'm sorry Caro. It's been one hell of a day.'
'That makes four this week, but who's counting?'
'It is the end of term, you know.'
'Oh yes. I had realized that.' A condemnation. Warning
bells sounded behind his aching eye. 'Three times every
year the air gets thick with martyrdom, and conversation
sparkles with chat about school plays and sports days,
examinations and reports. Sooner or later the message
does get through that the end of term is about to strike.'
He tested the water with a smile of propitiation.
'I'm sorry. Really I am.'
'What I just don't understand, Chris, is why you always
have to make such a production of it all.'
Sometimes Chris would wish that he had the capacity
to raise his voice and shout back — a thing he'd never been
able to do. Words spoken in uncontrolled anger were to
him words which could never be erased, no matter how
often Caroline assured him they didn't mean a thing.
'Look, Caro, I'm tired.'
'It comes round often enough in all conscience. There
must be thousands of teachers who manage to survive
without falling apart with exhaustion the way you always
do.'
He pushed his splayed fingers viciously against the
cream velvet pile; the parallel score marks gave him a
strange pleasure. 'Things will be better next week.'
'So now it's light at the end of the tunnel time?'
'Oh Caro, give it a rest. Please?'
'Or the syndrome of the penultimate week? The one
Hugh says drives strong men to drink?' A toss of the head,

perfectly executed. 'I'd never even heard of the word until I met you.'

Chris let a quick grin flit across his face.

'There were a lot of things you'd never experienced before you met me, my girl.'

A flash of answering mischief sparked and was extinguished. He decided to press home the advantage.

'I know I must be impossible to live with.'

A mistake. Caroline had no time for losers.

'That's true. Just thought I'd mention it. It's getting a bit monotonous.'

He let his head lie against the sofa back and closed his eyes. Caroline looked at him, finger rising to lip in the manner of a puzzled child. When she spoke again her tone was spontaneous, concerned.

'You meant it, didn't you? It really has been a bad day. More than usual?'

He opened his eyes and nodded.

'Maria Treadwell.' A flat announcement.

'That bright little girl whose father beat her up? The one who's taking eight O levels next year?'

'There's been a change of plan. She's going to have a baby instead.'

'But she's only fifteen, isn't she?'

'Yes. Something of a later developer by the standards of Barncroft Comprehensive.'

He looked up into troubled eyes; willed her to lessen the distance, both physical and emotional, between them.

'Chris, I'm sorry. What's going to happen to her?'

'God knows. The father appears to be Andrew Vickers, our grievous bodily harm merchant. Engaging young villain. Life hasn't been a bundle of fun for him either; in and out of care, in and out of court.' He glanced at the grandmother clock, hoisted himself stiffly to his feet. 'So I'd better take a quick shower if I'm going to get back in time.'

She tensed visibly and drew back. There had been no dissipation of anger, just a temporary deflection.

'Back where?'

'Back to school. Maria's mum finishes work at six and wants to see me. I *am* the child's form master.'

The defensive note was back again. Chris flinched.

'You're pathetic, Chris. You're a pushover for everyone who spins you a hard luck story—a walking doormat. Just as soon as they snap their fingers you come bounding to their side like a well-trained dog. People can get along without you, you know, even in Barncroft Comprehensive. You must really enjoy yourself playing Almighty God with other people's lives. All right.' Her voice began to rise. 'Go along and set the world to rights. Just don't expect that I'll always be sitting here waiting for you when you get back.'

Resentment and a sense of injustice fought against a recognition that some at least of what she'd said was valid. So far as his own pupils were concerned, that was.

He lowered his voice.

'I hope you realize that all the windows are wide open and the Pringles are probably lying back in their deck-chairs drinking in every word you say.'

'I don't care if the whole sodding neighbourhood is listening.'

Caroline, convent-educated, had an intense dislike of bad language and never used it. The significance of this would not strike Chris until many hours later.

'Look, I've got to go now, but I will get home just as soon as I can. Honestly.' What imp of perversity tempted him to make one final try at reconciliation? 'Just think, we break up for the summer on Wednesday. By Thursday night we'll be down at Treskellan.'

'Treskellan!' She almost spat the word.

'Now what have I said?'

Caroline looked at him thoughtfully, walked slowly

over to the window. She stood there, looking out, and spoke with quiet control.

'I'm not coming to Treskellan this year.'

'Not coming to Treskellan?'

'It's not obligatory, is it?'

'But we always go to Treskellan. Treskellan is home.'

'Correction. Treskellan is your home. It belongs to you and that bloody incestuous family of yours. I'm sick to death of the place.'

A muscle twitched in protest at the side of his mouth as Chris choked back his immediate retort.

'But we've only just bought Pendrufford!'

'Wrong again. You've just bought Pendrufford on the strength of your father's legacy. We've been going down there from time immemorial and I'm bored with it. I'm tired of basking in the reflected glory of being related by marriage to the sainted Dr Quinn. I'm sick of jolly sailing trips and evenings knocking back drinks with the locals in the Green Dragon.'

Grim-faced: 'I see.' He didn't see at all.

'The prospect of another dose of jovial Russell and dreary Melanie and dear little Alex is more than I can stomach.'

'It never seems to have bothered you before. You've asked Alex to stay here often enough.'

A flicker of indecision.

'She's all right, I suppose. But Alex is your sister, like Russell's your brother, and Melanie's your sister-in-law, and Angela's your niece, and Treskellan's your—'

'Yes, all right. You've made your point. Several times. You make us sound like latter-day Borgias.' He dropped a kiss on her forehead. It was like kissing his mother-in-law: a ritual duty enjoyed by neither. 'We'll talk about it when I get home.'

Sitting in the car, he fastened the seat-belt, started the engine, glanced back hopefully at the open door. His eyes encountered those of Mr Pringle, engaged in hoeing the next-door garden. The two men exchanged civil nods of greeting, neighbour fashion. Then the old man smiled and winked in a silent message of male commiseration.

Chris released the handbrake and drove off against the outrushing tide of commuter traffic.

High above the cliffs of the north Cornish coast Toby Wilde scrambled up the dusty path between banks of bramble and gorse, his feet slipping badly on the scree. His heavy hornrimmed glasses were steaming over, his breathing heavy and laboured, the muscles at the back of his calves beginning to tighten in protest. His year of intensive study might have gained him a licence to work, but it had done little for his physical fitness.

At the top of the hill he leant back against a massive boulder encrusted with lichen and allowed his heaving chest to settle. He fought off a wave of vertigo as he peered over a cleft in the rocks to a great tumbled mass of shattered granite blocks two hundred feet below, washed over and caressed by gently creaming waters. Already the fierce heat from the sun was dying as it moved down towards the west, and a soft breeze had begun to ripple through the spears of ripening corn in the field behind him.

Toby mopped his face and neck; polished his glasses and replaced them; drew a large-scale ordnance map from the hip pocket of his bright blue shorts.

It had been a long day. Not that it was all that far from Surrey, but the firm's car which Mr Foxen had lent him was overdue for superannuation and had proved a temperamental creature with little enthusiasm for the lure of the open road. Nor did it do a lot for the image of the bright young business executive type he'd thought of presenting to Alex. But then, anyone who had opted to remain a perpetual student to the age of twenty-five was well accustomed to financial stringency. Even penury. The great thing was to carry it off in style.

This was the first holiday he'd ever spent behind the wheel of a car. He had travelled widely on the Continent by hitching, by hiking, even by cycling, always with a sleeping-bag and rucksack on his back. By comparison, a tour of his native country with a suitcase in the boot and a bed to sleep in was a considerable step up the social ladder. He was no longer just a bright young man with dark curly hair and glasses, clean-cut and good-looking, but a qualified solicitor as well. That should impress Alex; on second thoughts, he was not so sure. The law was a little bit like accountancy: safe and dull. All that conveyancing, with the odd will from time to time; perhaps the occasional intestacy to provide a spot of light relief. For the next forty years.

A depressing thought. There had been a long period in his teens when Toby had been intent on becoming, one day, the greatest detective the Metropolitan Police had ever known. No other career had ever entered his head, and it came as a devastating blow to his self-esteem when, despite being armed with every possible attribute in the way of interest and qualifications, the police had rejected him on the grounds of defective eyesight. He'd effectively wasted two full years before settling for the vicarious attractions of the law, and taken up articles with the silver-haired Mr Foxen.

Now those five years were over, and he had passed his finals. His job was secured. He would wear dark suits and a collar and tie; learn to play squash; get elected to the Round Table; might even put up for membership of the golf-club.

Meanwhile — he scanned the map with a frown — he ought to be somewhere close to Treskellan. Well past Padstow — ah! He'd found Port Laverock, where he was booked in for bed and breakfast. Track back from there.

Right, he'd found it. Quite a small village apparently, but at least another mile or so's walk up and down the tortuous coastal path.

He wondered what young Alex would say when he walked back into her life. She'd been in her first year at Guildford when he'd been doing Part I at law school. A nice child, refreshingly different from most of the strident feminist lobby then in residence. Lively, with a certain wanton innocence. No messing about either, not with Alex. They had argued a lot, he remembered, but without heat or the giving of offence. They'd had a lot of fun together.

Four, nearly five years ago.

He glanced at his watch, then down at his crumpled shorts, his perspiring feet; looked back across the fields to the distant car park holding a multicoloured confection of Dinky toys glinting metallically in the evening sun. It was half past five—a bit late. Best, perhaps, to go back, find his digs, wash and change? Ring her up?

Always provided, of course, that she still lived in this part of the world. The exchange of Christmas cards had lapsed, as had so many others, after the first year. Yes, better to telephone first even if it did spoil the surprise.

His landlady was short and round, warm and welcoming. She handed him the local directory and shut the door to give him privacy. Only one Quinn was listed: Dr S. J. Quinn. Two numbers: one for Goldenacre—that was the place—and one for the surgery. He rang Goldenacre.

The voice that answered was attractive and husky without a trace of soft West Country accent. Not Alex.

'Good evening. I wonder if I might speak to Miss Alexis Quinn?' All very stilted and polite.

A pause.

'I'm sorry, but Alex doesn't live here now.'

Toby's excitement died away, leaving an emptiness of disappointment which surprised him.

'Oh.' He felt the voice deserved an explanation. 'I

didn't know. Sorry to have troubled you.'

'Wait a minute. Is it urgent?'

'Well, not exactly. It's just that I'm on a touring holiday, and Alex and I were students together some years
back. Being over at Port Laverock, I thought I might look
her up.'

'No problem.' What a nice lady! 'Dr Quinn died last
year and Alex moved out. She's got a place of her own
now, only it's not on the phone.' The voice grew more
guarded. 'She would remember you, I expect?'

Time to produce his credentials. The modest
approach.

'I'd like to think so. My name's Wilde. Toby Wilde. We
used to sing madrigals together.'

'Did you now?' There was a suppressed gurgle, a quick
apology. 'I'm sorry. Look, why don't you give Melanie a
ring?'

'Melanie?'

'Of course her number isn't in the book yet either. It's
chaotic down here at the moment with all of us moving
house and the new directory not due out for months yet.
I'm only glad you haven't got summer diarrhœa.
Melanie's Russell's wife—Alex's brother you know. Just
moved to a place called The Shrubberies up on Meadowbank—Mafia Mews as we call it.' Toby frowned in concentration. 'She'll be home from work by now I should
think and can send Angela down with a message. Oh no,
Angela's tied up being Titania. But don't worry. It'll be
all right, and Alex can ring you back or something.'

All hopes of a delightful evening of nostalgia in some
quiet pub with the fair Alexis that night receded fast.

'That would be very kind of you, Miss—'

'It's Mrs, actually. Hyson. Susanne Hyson.'

'Mrs Hyson. I take it you know Alex? Personally?'

'Of course. Everyone knows Alex.' She laughed. 'Everyone knows everyone in a place like this.'

'She's not married or anything?'

'No, Mr Wilde, she has not married.'

'Or anything?'

A distinct pause.

'Or anything, so far as I know.'

'Great. So if you would let me have Melanie — Mrs Quinn's number?'

He wrote it down in ballpoint on the back of his hand. 'I'm very grateful. Thank you.'

'No trouble. You get on to Melanie. She'll sort things out. Very competent lady, our Melanie. Good luck, Mr Wilde.'

It was not until he had replaced the receiver that it occurred to Toby that Mrs Hyson could quite easily have given him Alex's new address. He gave a wry smile. His credentials were going to be checked before he got within shouting distance of Alex. Mrs Hyson was quite a shrewd lady herself.

Maria Treadwell's mother was already waiting in the classroom: an ageing woman in her early thirties, ill at ease, clearly apprehensive.

Chris shook hands, felt his jaw tightening under the smile he kept for first meetings with unknown or belligerent parents. Mrs Treadwell perched upright on the edge of a grey moulded stacking chair. Her dress, like that of her children, was adequate but drab. She had been dainty once, possibly quite pretty, but now her face was grey and lined, her blue eyes sullen and defensive. Not very bright, Chris guessed, but shrewd with the survival instinct endemic in the district, never prepared to admit defeat by grinding poverty and lack of hope. This would be the first time she had ever visited the school to talk about her children.

Not for the first time, he speculated about the identity of Maria's real father. The younger Treadwell children had both been placed in remedial classes soon after arrival, but Maria was possessed of a quick intelligence which had delighted him. Lively, pert and pretty, Maria had long ago become his favourite pupil in so far as he would admit to such a lapse from professional ethics. It was she who presented him with the occasional bonus of reassurance that teaching history in Barncroft Comprehensive was not entirely a waste of time.

Now all his hopes, his belief that here was one girl who could emerge from this scrapyard of academic aspiration, were over. Maria was programmed to become yet another of the schoolgirl mothers over whom television documentaries were prone to agonize.

Mrs Treadwell had begun to talk, in rapid staccato bursts of disconnection.

She had been upset of course. But she'd stand by her girl. None of that going down the hospital to get her fixed up. Didn't hold with that. Didn't hold with it at all. She'd had five herself. Not all of them exactly wanted, that she would admit. But who was she to say they didn't have a right to their own life? Wicked it was, what young girls got up to nowadays. Downright wicked.

Chris found himself smiling without effort. He was beginning to warm to Mrs Treadwell.

She'd been down the Welfare and found out about Maria's rights. They called them one-parent families these days, too. Much nicer, really, than it used to be when a girl got into trouble.

Her eyelids dropped suddenly, twin curtains drawn over tired eyes, and Chris was confirmed in his suspicions that the Mr Treadwell now serving time for assaulting his children was not the real father of the girl Maria.

The silence became unbearable. He brought her back.

Maria's schooling, sir? Well, it was a shame she'd have to leave, seeing she'd done so well. But that was life, wasn't it?

Against all his inclinations, Chris found himself nodding. Any comment about the tragic waste of talent and opportunity seemed inappropriate. Mrs Treadwell was the person who would have to cope, and she had seen it all before.

'If there is anything at all I can do—'

The classic overture of well-intentioned impotence in time of other people's troubles.

'That's very kind of you, sir.'

Overture rejected out of hand.

'And I would just like to thank you for all you've done for Maria. She's ever so upset—feels she's let you down. So we thought it best she doesn't come back to school. So near the end of term, like.'

She stood up, pulled a brown cardigan round thin shoulders, picked up her handbag.

Chris rose, impelled to put an affectionate hand on those shoulders, to convey something of shared understanding, good wishes, admiration. Instead he performed the formal handshake and watched her leave: moving with the stoic acceptance of one who had never known any reason to believe that something better might turn up some day.

The evening sunlight streaked in speckled bands across the clutter of desks, thick with sparkling dandruff of chalk and dust, filtered and distorted by warped and broken Venetian blinds which splayed out in fans from ropes holding them in bunches high out of reach. Chris liked to think there might be some apt symbolism in their regular destruction: a healthy protest of the young against incarceration in purpose-built boxes where even a glimpse of the outside world was circumscribed by parallel bars of plastic grey.

He sat down and slumped over his desk, mind thrown out of gear, thoughts disjointed. Despair gave way to anger, anger to sadness, sadness to resignation. The only response? Perhaps Mrs Treadwell was wiser than she knew.

Melanie was just getting out of the bath when the telephone began to ring. She pulled on a towelling bathrobe of olive green and padded down to answer it. When she came back she was smiling happily.

She pulled off her plastic shower cap and started to unwind pink rollers from her hair. What a lovely week it had been! Glorious weather, the last of her new furniture delivered, and now this nice young man wanting to get in touch with Alex. It would do the child good to meet a fresh face for a change.

It would be lovely to have a small party; the first she would have held in the new home. She'd been saving up the proper housewarming until Christopher came down, but that wouldn't be till next week. Friday would be best really, so that Geoff would just have time to make it before he went home.

She wandered through to the bedroom. It would have been nice to have had a proper en suite bathroom, but then, one couldn't have everything one wanted in this life. And the master bedroom was lovely—big picture windows facing south and west, giving an even better view of the cliffs and bays away to the west than they got from the lounge patio downstairs.

Russell had let her design the bedroom exactly as she wanted. Rich cream wallpaper and matching curtains and covered duvet in dark brown with a sort of orange geometrical design, very contemporary; and a big white fitted unit with gilt handles which provided all the wardrobe and drawer space she was ever likely to need. It took up the whole of one wall and even had concealed lighting round the mirror.

She sat on a fluffy brown stool and began to file away at her nails. Alex could make all the funny remarks she liked about the new Meadowbank Estate now nearing completion above the village, but Melanie simply loved living there. They had named their house The Shrubberies—a spacious villa built on quite the finest plot, right at the end overlooking the sea. It was such a pity the locals had taken to calling the new development Mafia Mews, but that was probably because most of the houses had been sold to prosperous business people from up country, strangers who only came down for a few weeks each year, making the place look a bit desolate at times.

Still, it would be better next week when the schools broke up and families could get away on holiday. And the builders had promised to make up the private road before the winter set in. That would make it look much better.

She spread her fingers, frowning a little at the state of her hands. Using that cream Susanne had recommended didn't seem to be making much difference. But then, her fingers had always been squat and sturdy—hardworking hands, she always said. Never could get on with those rubber gloves; they stuck to her hands and smelt quite disgusting. Nor would she ever want to employ a woman to do her housework, no matter what Russell said: poking and prying and telling her neighbours all your personal business.

She must be old-fashioned, but she'd always enjoyed cooking and housework, even before Russell started to do so well and they were able to afford to buy labour-saving gadgets. Just like she enjoyed entertaining friends and going out to meals with them in the evening.

Tonight they were going to see Angela playing Titania in the school play. She'd look quite lovely in the part, being so slight and slim. Susanne had said in the salon that morning that she and Stan had been most impressed by the opening performance. And Geoff would be going with Alex tomorrow night. Nice for the child to have support in the audience on each of the nights. She might be fourteen but she still needed to know that her family cared about her.

She heard Russell's car draw up outside. Ran a comb through her hair, smiled at her reflection in the mirror and tightened the belt around her waist as she went out to meet him.

Russell was already bounding up the stairs with all the enthusiasm of a large and friendly dog: a big broad man radiating confidence and good-nature.

'Putting on the war paint, then?' He gave her a quick kiss and a hug. 'You haven't run all the hot water, have you?'

'Of course not, darling. But could you just manage to pop down to Shrimp Cottage first? There's been a phone message for Alex. I'll run your bath while you're away.'

'Of course. What's it all about?'

Melanie's pale blue eyes lit up.

'Well, it's rather fun. This young man phoned. Toby Wilde, he said his name was. Very well-spoken and polite. Knew Alex when she was at University a year or two back. I've never heard her mention him, have you? So I said perhaps they might like to meet here for a few drinks on Saturday. Then we can ask Susanne and Stan, and Geoff too, of course. Have a sort of party.'

Russell put his hands on his wife's shoulders and smiled at her excitement.

'I think you're wonderful. It's a great idea.'

She looked a trifle anxious.

'You do think Alex will be pleased, don't you?'

'Well, she certainly ought to be. Where's this boy staying?'

'At Port Laverock.'

'Yes, but where?'

Melanie's eyes widened. 'I've no idea. I never thought to ask him.'

'You mean you didn't even get his phone number?' He

let out a low whistle. 'I mean to say, it's a bit tough on the lad if he's got to wait till Saturday—two whole days.'

'But Russell, she's pretty tied up with Geoff at the moment, and they're going to the school play tomorrow night.'

'Melanie darling—' his voice was gentle— 'Alex is free all day, you know, and Geoff would understand. She might have liked to meet this Toby sooner than Saturday.'

'Oh dear, do you think she might be just a bit upset?'

'Of course not,' he said with perfect honesty. If Russell was sure of one thing, it was that his sister would be absolutely livid.

When a lady bearing brooms and dusters barged her way into the classroom Chris was fast asleep over his desk. He rubbed his eyes and laughed politely at the very idea that he had no home to go to, before making a rapid escape. He did not feel bright enough for any prolonged exchange of cheery badinage.

He drove home automatically and was turning off into Chandlers Grove when he remembered he had said he'd hurry home. A split second later he remembered why.

Dear God in heaven! He had actually forgotten the entire incident. Was there time enough to work out exactly what had happened?

Caroline had said she would not go to Treskellan, not in any heated outburst of anger, but quite calmly as though she had been thinking about it for some time. But if she had, she should have felt able to discuss this with him, if only he'd been less absorbed with other things. Considerably more worrying was the way she'd talked about Russell and the others, in a way calculated to hurt. Caroline could be waspish at times, but rarely with malice, and whatever their faults, his family were fond of her. So this was quite out of character, and delivered not as a cheap jibe in a fit of temper, but as a statement of fact.

Something quite serious must have happened.

Perhaps he was over-reacting. Perhaps she would dash out to meet him full of remorse and admit she'd been upset and angry and was only trying to get her own back. That, at least, would be in character, and the whole thing could be forgotten.

But when he got home, she wasn't there.

There was just a note propped against the phone: *Since you can't be bothered to come home I've gone round to Helen's. Will probably stay the night. Food in the fridge.*

Helen? Who the devil was Helen?

Irritation seized him first, quickly replaced by a wave of unashamed relief that there were to be no more scenes that night; no more sensibilities to be considered. Tomorrow would be time enough for all that.

Chris ran a bath, undressed and sank gratefully into deep warm water; put his mind back into neutral.

An hour later he was asleep.

The big house known as Goldenacre stood in more than an acre of garden above the village, screened from the adjacent Meadowbank Estate by a thick wall of golden leylandia. It was an expression both of Victorian craftsmanship and values, being solid, sound and splendid. Over a century of weathering had rendered it mellow and beautiful in a setting of spacious lawn and massive trees: copper beech and silver birch, oak and elm.

Round the wavy edges of the lawn were wide beds of flowers and shrubs, the whole backed by a steeply shelving bluff banked with rhododendrons and azaleas. On the northern boundary a busy stream rushed down a deep rift in the rock-face to the sea.

The house had been for generations associated with the long and benevolent reign of Dr Quinn. Here his children had been born and here his wife had died after the birth of the youngest child, Alexis. Over the years the sick and troubled from miles around had made their way up the hill, seeking the healing powers and jovial reassurance for which he was renowned. When it was too late for healing, they were helped to discover the courage and serenity they sought.

From all accounts the old man had been nothing if not flamboyant, delighting in an affection and respect that verged on adulation. Rumour had it that his extravagant lifestyle had outstripped his income for many years, a rumour substantiated by the amount of his estate. There seemed to be precious little left apart from the house itself, as everyone soon found out from the local weekly: a newspaper as diligent in publishing details of people's wills as in listing every mourner at local funerals. In the case of Dr Quinn, the list had filled two entire columns of tiny print.

Susanne Hyson had not been around to feel the shockwaves of indignation that rocked the village when Goldenacre was put on the market within weeks of the old man's death. But she had no illusions at all about the suspicion and fine-honed hostility lying in wait for any purchaser who dared set foot in the doctor's house.

The Hysons had fallen under the spell of Goldenacre at first sight and had made an immediate offer to buy it as it stood: furniture, fittings, the lot. Stan had the foresight to realize that if they were going to commit any form of sacrilege, it had best be done at once, before they arrived to take up residence. Not that there was much they had wanted to change. The old surgery was replaced by a conservatory, but a modernized kitchen and a couple of bathrooms had been the only other alterations. From the outside, at least, nothing seemed changed when they moved in early in the year.

The initial hatred had been tangible, frightening. The

only people they'd already met were two of the vendors, the children of the late doctor. Russell had always been friendly, and his wife Melanie very pleasant. It was Alex who remained distant for a very long time; but then Goldenacre had always been her home and Susanne knew it must hurt like hell to see strangers in possession.

The thaw had not really set in until she'd taken over the village hairdressing salon down in Fore Street. She'd closed the place down for a couple of weeks to refit and decorate, opening again for the start of the season at Easter. With Melanie to help her, and no competition this side of Port Laverock, things began to improve. It was amazing how intimacies became established under the dryer, and how the most frigid of clients felt constrained to make conversation under comb and scissors.

Susanne rose from her deckchair and whistled sharply. 'Come on, Jezebel! How about a nice run along the sand dunes?'

A golden labrador came charging down from the rhododendrons and braked in a scatter of gravel at her feet.

'Time to go dig our lord and master out of the nineteenth hole before they throw him out, my girl.'

Jezebel raced ahead towards the narrow path which ran alongside the stream on its way down to the sea; fidgeted with impatience while her mistress exchanged a few remarks with Alex Quinn in the garden of her cottage at its mouth, and streaked ahead over the dunes beyond the last of the houses. The sun was setting in a rosy fluff of pink cotton-wool away on the horizon and a cool breeze had begun to blow off the sea. A beautiful evening.

Stan was on the point of leaving as they reached the clubhouse: a tall spare man in his fifties, grey-haired and bearded, immaculate in navy, a white collar showing over his fine wool guernsey; tanned and fit; good white teeth.

He gave Susanne a quick hug, quieted the excited dog. 'Glad you came. I've missed you.'

'And so you should. A day of shampooing and setting and an evening of catching up with the ironing while you swan around sailing clubs and golf-courses indulging in dissolute living—there's no justice any more.'

'But I like living on your moral earnings. I'm retired, remember? It was you who wanted to launch out into big business.'

'True. But think how bored we'd be if we were stuck with each other every day.'

He looked down at her fondly, grey eyes twinkling.

'Never that, my love.'

Susanne felt her eyes misting and blinked crossly.

'I do rather love you, you know; even though I know it's only my body you're after. Thank God.'

'That's true. Why d'you think I have to play all that golf and tennis when you're out at work? Sublimation of my erotic energies, that's what it is.'

'Fool.' She took his hand and started to run with him along the shore. Both were out of breath by the time they reached the harbour wall.

'Pax!' cried the man. 'I'm not a match for you and Jez any more. Let's have a breather. Tell me the latest news from your hotbed of indiscretion.'

'Oh!' She clapped her hand to her mouth. 'I forgot. Though it's nothing to do with the salon. I had an intriguing phone call from a mysterious stranger tonight.'

Stan looked up quickly, eyebrows raised.

'No, darling, not that kind of stranger. It's a bit of Alex's past that's turned up this time. Made a nice change from all those medical emergencies who keep ringing up still. An ex-boy-friend. So I put him on to Melanie.'

'That wasn't very charitable. Why didn't you ask him over? Take him down to Alex yourself?'

'Actually, I never thought of it. But now Melanie's gone straight into one of her gracious living kicks and invited the poor devil to drinks and things on toast on

Saturday. She phoned just before I left. We're invited too.'

Stan laughed. 'Serves you right.'

'You're a heartless brute, Stan Hyson. And of course Alex is fuming with rage, muttering dark imprecations against people who go interfering in other people's affairs without ever consulting them.'

'I expect Melanie meant well.'

'Oh, I'm sure of it. She always does. She's the kindest woman I've ever known. Heart of gold and all that. Which is why Alex just goes on grinding her teeth and saying nothing to her.'

'Melanie's been very good to us,' he reminded her.

'I know.' Susanne tried to look contrite and failed. 'Just imagine how that poor lad must feel having to meet the assembled Quinns and assorted friends when all he wanted was a pint and a nostalgic chat with Alex.'

Stan didn't answer. Susanne looked up to see him staring out to sea with a faraway look in his eyes. She put an arm round his waist.

'Stan? Come back, please?'

He gave a little start.

'You like it here, don't you Sue?'

'I love it. I love the house, I love my job, I love the village, and I love you. I think I'm becoming a sentimental slob. I've never been so happy in all my life. How about you?'

He cupped her face in his hands.

'I'm the luckiest man in the world. But there's something I must tell you: a small cloud on the horizon.'

A quick surge of alarm.

'Tell me, Stan.'

'I've just seen Adrian. Coming out of the caravan site. About half an hour ago.'

Colour drained from her face in little waves.

'But I thought he'd gone back to London.'

'Yes.'

She shivered suddenly.

'Stan?'

'Yes, love?'

'I think I'm going to be sick.'

CHAPTER 2. FRIDAY

Friday morning was bright and sunny. Caroline swung her shining red Fiat on to the M3 at Bagshot, trod hard on the accelerator and zoomed out into the overtaking lane. The wind from the open sunroof blew her hair back over her face as the exhilaration of speed recharged the batteries of her vitality.

By lunch-time she should be in Bournemouth with her parents. A brilliant idea. As her mother had said on the phone, gently reproachful, they saw far too little of her in the summer when the garden was at its best. She was much too delighted to add that the reason they'd brought her a car of her own was as a tactful invitation to visit them more often. Caroline had hedged about her precise time of arrival and begged her mother not to go to any special trouble. A waste of time, of course. Mrs Barrett would already be polishing the furniture, airing the sheets and have sent Dad off to the shops for special delicacies for the occasion.

Caroline needed time to think before taking on the role of prodigal daughter. Helen had served her purpose. She'd been something of a parasite all through the course on flower arrangement they'd both attended: one of those lonely women of indeterminate age who was always begging her to call round one evening — an invitation Caroline had managed to evade with some skill.

Circumstances, however, dictated events. Helen could

provide the only sanctuary she could think of where Chris was an unknown quantity. The price demanded was high. A long evening spent making valuable contributions to a conversation about the proper rearing of house plants; and the tremendous fun one could have with window-boxes.

Helen had a flat. The flat had a spare bedroom. So what could be more natural than, the moment Caroline discovered, late in the evening, that she had mislaid her key to Chandlers Grove, that she should be invited to spend the night? Better still, to spend the weekend, with Chris being away on a dreary teacher's conference. They might spend Saturday at Kew Gardens. A sobering thought.

It was fortunate that Helen had to go off to her job at the local library in the morning. Directly she'd left after a breakfast high in bran and vitamin C, Caroline scribbled a note of appreciation, explaining how she'd found the missing key in the lining of her handbag, and promising to be in touch again very soon.

It had taken no time at all to go back home, ring her mother and pack a suitcase. It would be good to have a long weekend in which to think.

What was she going to do about Chris? Helen had been easy, but he was a very different proposition: casual, easy-going, a very private person, irritating, honest to a fault, but gullible — never.

If only she'd never become involved in that rotten business down at Treskellan in the first place. A few drinks too many, a bit of lightheadedness — that was all it was. The memory — and for months she had managed to shut the whole incident behind one of the closed doors in her mind — was even now enough to send a wave of warm colour to stain her cheeks. Now someone else held the key to that locked door and, it seemed, fully intended to use it. Caroline would never have believed it possible, not in a thousand years.

She could always tell Chris the truth: he'd be shocked and hurt of course, but at least there would be an end of it. It was she who would have to submit to all the shame and humiliation, and that was a prospect she could not possibly entertain. There had to be a better way.

Deny the whole thing? She'd never been any good at lying, especially to Chris. Anyhow, it would be impossible, in view of the evidence—evidence of whose existence Caroline had been completely unaware: until now. She could claim that she had been just a victim, an unwilling or unwitting victim? That might work.

Funny how you could misjudge people: people that you knew and trusted; people you had never harmed in any way at all.

She overtook two large container lorries, realized that her teeth were clenched hard. Chris hadn't believed that she was sick to death of Treskellan, and why should he? It wasn't true. She had been wildly excited when they'd managed to buy the small stone house at Pendrufford Point, couldn't wait to begin work on transforming it into the dream cottage they'd been planning all year. What a mess it all was.

'Blast!' She checked her speed as the high signs heralding the end of the motorway flashed overhead. She'd missed her customary turn-off for Bournemouth. She grinned ruefully. Some Freudian significance, perhaps? Her sub-conscious mind directing her towards the more familiar route down to Treskellan?

And why not? Her eyes lit up. Why not indeed? At least make some last ditch attempt to have the evidence de-stroyed? Even destroy it herself? What a marvellous idea! Why on earth hadn't she thought of it before?

Her eyes sparkled with excitement. The adrenalin began to surge, her spirits to quicken; that would be

much more her style than cringing in terror before
uncertainty.

Just ahead lay the elongated roundabout which presented
the choice: south to Salisbury and Hampshire, or west to
Exeter and Cornwall.

She didn't make it the first time round. Slim brown
hands clenched on the steering-wheel, she made a complete
circuit before starting round again. The second time
there was no hesitation. With indicator flashing, she took
the sharp corner, allowed the wheel to slide in a sensual
caressing spin back through her hands, and straightened
out on the narrow wooded road ahead. Exeter, said the
signpost, 114 miles.

Her mother would be disappointed, of course. But she
could always phone her from a garage somewhere. Caroline
was on her way to Treskellan.

This was not, as it turned out, a decision she would live
to regret.

Fore Street was a terrace of grey stone cottages which
hugged the shoreline from the harbour as far as the
stream which plunged down through the cliff from Goldenacre. Neat and bright with a riot of flowering shrubs in
minuscule front gardens, all had hanging baskets of
geraniums and lobelia and were fronted by low granite
walls sprouting valerian, aubrietia and nasturtiums.

At the harbour end, next door to the Green Dragon,
was Susanne's, its tiny forecourt paved to allow for the
parking of prams and pushchairs. It was debatable which
of the two establishments had the greater claim as a
centre for sociable gathering and gossip. As Susanne's
clientele was predominantly female, it was natural that
conversation centred on medical debate, scandal and indiscretion, leavened by that indelicate indulgence in
earthy humour which flourishes only when women con-
gregate with their own sex.

Local men reserved their patronage almost exclusively for late night opening on Fridays, when they would cluster together for protection and exchange serious talk about Plymouth Argyle and engine maintenance. The staff was not expected to participate in these discussions but only to provide the service for which it was paid: which enabled Susanne to cope on her own and allow Melanie to go home at five.

Melanie would not have been Susanne's first choice of assistant in the salon, but she had been part of the deal, along with the fixtures and fittings as an existing, if part-time, member of staff. She wasn't really sufficiently qualified to lighten the load, having abandoned her apprenticeship before marrying Russell. Nor did she do a lot for the image Susanne's was trying to present, with her shapeless clothes and passion for woollen cardigans, every one lovingly knitted by hand.

On the other hand, Melanie had gone out of her way to be kind to the Hysons, and was in other ways a tower of strength. She knew everybody and had been generous and loyal in helping Susanne to be accepted by customers who came into the shop. She was the soul of discretion, knowing instinctively how to adjust her manner appropriately to each of their regular customers; she could be lively and cheerful, or kind and sympathetic as the occasion demanded, and was probably in receipt of most of the more intimate confidences.

She was also far better able than Susanne herself to withstand the draining of nervous energy imposed by the perpetually disgruntled, and the occasionally ill-mannered.

On balance, the arrangement worked pretty well.

Susanne took old Mrs Martin's arm and helped her out of her seat and over to the bank of dryers; put her walking stick close at hand and offered her the latest issue of her favourite magazine. For the last half-hour she had listened in sympathy to a distressed monologue on Mrs Martin's latest visit to hospital which had scared the old lady very much.

Susanne smiled and patted her hand. She'd grown very fond of the indomitable, frightened old lady, and wished she could do more.

'You look tired.' Melanie had leapt to Mrs Martin's vacated seat and was polishing round the basin and mirror with her usual vigour. 'You wouldn't like me to stay on this evening, would you?'

Susanne flopped on to a chair.

'Bless you, Melanie, but I'm not tired. Just a bit depressed. It must be dreadful to be old and frail, don't you think?'

'It will happen to all of us one day, I expect.'

'Really scary, isn't it? Anyhow, we're not too busy for the rest of the afternoon. Tonight it's just the usual short back and sides brigade. One day—' her eyes lit up— 'I'll get one of them to let me do a decent styling job—it only needs one to set the trend, at least among the younger men. So far a blow wave seems to strike them as the ultimate in decadence. Who's next?'

As Melanie moved over to consult the appointments book the door was pushed open. Susanne looked up, her professional smile of welcome switching rapidly from lips to eyes.

'Alex!'

A short slim bundle of energy erupted through the doorway, blonde flyaway hair pushed back from freckled snub-nosed face. In habitual T-shirt and jeans, she looked absurdly young for a girl of twenty-three.

'Can I come in?' She waved and sent a beaming smile towards the old lady under the dryer. 'Isn't it coffee time yet?'

'Be our guest. The kettle's on, and you know where the makings are.' Susanne cast a despairing look at her visitor. 'Alex—your hair! Why won't you let me do something with it? On the house? It could be lovely if you ever bothered with it.'

The girl backed off defensively.

'Now don't start that again. I don't come in here to be insulted.'

'You don't come in here at all, except for coffee and a chat. Very conservative lot, you Treskellans.'

'I'm just not the slinky type, Susanne. Anyway, you people scare me to death once you get a pair of scissors in your hands. You get carried away. I'd be half scalped before I knew what was happening, with Melanie scooping it all up with her little dustpan and brush.'

Susanne laughed and shrugged. Her hands itched to turn this coltish young tearaway into something quite different. But then she would no longer be Alex, would she? It was amazing how people's appearance reflected their personality, she thought, looking idly at Melanie.

'You mean you don't want to impress this boy-friend of yours tomorrow night?'

With a quick glance to see if Melanie were watching, Alex made a face at her.

'No,' she said shortly. 'Anyhow, Toby's never been a boy-friend, not in the way you mean. He's just a guy I used to know.'

'A boy-friend whom you sang madrigals with?'

'It was a club, for goodness sake! He's got a very good voice. We didn't lie under the stars singing duets in the moonlight, if that's what you think.'

'Shame. Never mind, I'm still looking forward to meeting him. I'm sure it's going to be a lovely party.'

Melanie smiled with pleasure, and Susanne felt properly ashamed. Neither she nor Alex would ever set out to hurt Melanie's feelings. Alex had vanished next door and could be heard dealing with the coffee.

'Oh, I do hope so,' said the older woman, 'to make up

for having to wait so long. I never thought of asking the young man which hotel he was in until Russell mentioned it. I'm really sorry, Alex.'

'Don't give it a thought, milove.' She planted a mug of coffee firmly in front of her sister-in-law and took a second one across to Mrs Martin. 'I keep telling you, he's just someone I used to know. No great romantic entanglement or anything.'

Melanie looked disappointed.

'Such a pity that Chris and Caroline won't be there as well. Then it would have been a real family party.'

Alex and Susanne picked up their mugs, avoiding one another's eyes.

'Yes,' said Alex carefully. 'Toby would have loved that, I'm sure. Look, I really called in to check about tonight. *Midsummer Night's Dream* and all that. How would it be if Geoff and I bring Angela back to my place after the show? Then she can spend the night with me, and you won't have to stop up waiting for her.'

Melanie's brow crinkled. 'Well, it's kind of you Alex, but there's really no need.'

'But you said it would be after eleven before we got home, and you've got the party to prepare for tomorrow. I'll see she gets a hearty breakfast and everything, if that's what's bothering you.'

Melanie hesitated. 'Well, perhaps. I should ask Angela. She often goes riding quite early on Saturdays. I wouldn't like her to get you up before you usually do.'

Alex tightened her lips. 'Fair enough. Just thought I'd offer. Anyhow, you've got a customer coming. Thanks for the coffee. Take care.'

The final dismissal bell of the day reverberated along the school corridors, followed on the instant by slamming doors, clattering footsteps and the clamour of voices. School was over for another week.

Hard on the heels of the pupils came the staff, grim-faced and weary in the tradition of every Friday afternoon. Today was added an extra dimension: the hunted look of those already close to exhaustion who had allowed themselves to fall behind with their annual returns, reports, registers.

Hugh Purcell, small and sprightly head of maths, made straight for the sink in the corner of the room and aimed a jet of water with practised skill from a green rubber spout attached to the tap into an electric kettle.

'Coffee, Chris?'

'Please.'

'Not going home tonight?'

'Not yet. Still got some work to do.' There had been no reply to his three phone calls home. Caroline would have to wait.

Hugh spooned instant coffee into a couple of green mugs heavily stained inside, picked up a bottle half full of milk and sniffed at it suspiciously.

'Chris, I'm sorry about that Maria Treadwell business. Know how you must feel. Super little girl. Could have gone far, given half a chance.'

Chris nodded.

'Yes. Saw her mum last night. She's withdrawing her from school. Done it already. She won't be coming back. I was thinking of writing to her. You know, good luck and all that. God knows she's going to need some.'

Hugh spun round.

'Are you out of your mind? Take it from me, old son, abandon any such thoughts before you live to regret them.'

'Why on earth?'

'Good God, you poor innocent fool! Shades of Lolita! Don't risk it, my boy. Don't even think of it. Imagine the headlines: "Middle-aged schoolmaster—" '

'I'm thirty-two!'

' "Middle-aged schoolmaster's letters to pregnant school-girl." You can't be that stupid!'

'You're not suggesting—?'

'I'm not suggesting a thing. It's how other people construe these things. Never put your emotions in writing, least of all to a schoolgirl mum for whom you had a particular affection. Oh yes you did. Avuncular affection I know, but affection none the less. Resist all temptation to commit your parting sentiments to paper.'

Chris sighed. 'Perhaps you're right. I would like to have seen her, though. Wish her well or something.'

'Forget it, Chris. Here, take your coffee and turn that creative imagination of yours in the direction of end of term reports. Your comments may be travesties of the truth, but at least they won't land you in court.'

Adrian Sheppard settled back more comfortably into the haystack, reflecting that this particular holiday promised to be successful beyond his wildest dreams. In every respect. The sexy little piece who'd picked him up at the dance last night—all heavy mascara and dangling earrings—was decidedly going to be a bit of all right. Tracey Harman she was called, with the body of a Russian gymnast. Amazing how different she looked now, lying beside him in school uniform. Swore she was sixteen, though he had his doubts. Whatever her age, Tracey had certainly been around.

As well as being at school, she had a Saturday job at Susanne's, the hairdressing salon in Fore Street. That might be useful; very useful indeed.

He detached his lips from her right ear, removed a wisp of dark hair from his tongue, and tried to get a little more matey.

'Here—what d'you think you're up to?'

The indignation was bold but simulated. You could always tell. He treated her to his special smile and kept his voice warm and reassuring. Adrian was good at that. He'd had a lot of practice.

'I bet you're a right little raver when you get going.'

She wriggled provocatively.

'You've got a lovely skin, Tracey. Like satin — all smooth and silky. It's such a pity to keep it all covered over, don't you think?'

Her eyes sparkled: a pleased child. 'You did know I'd be coming straight off the school bus. We've got to wear these boring dresses.'

'Let's get rid of it then, shall we?'

She pushed him away, apprehension in her eyes. 'What, in broad daylight? You must be joking!'

'No one can see us.'

'Look — what do you think I am? You needn't think that just because you bought me a couple of drinks — '

Time to retrench.

'But I don't, Tracey. I'm mighty particular who I lie down in haystacks with. I don't make a habit of this sort of thing.'

Tracey giggled. 'Me neither.'

Adrian sighed. Whatever Tracey's obvious talents were, sophisticated conversation was not going to be among them.

'I'm quite sure you don't.' She'd believe anything if he played his cards right. 'I think you're rather special.'

She eyed him from beneath lowered lashes. 'You're not so bad yourself.'

He wasn't either. Broad-shouldered, slim-hipped, lovely teeth. Very smooth operator, with a bit of class. A cut above most of the local talent. Plenty of money too, and didn't seem to mind spending it.

She sat up and began to brush her skirt free of grass. 'You're not going?'

'Got to. I've got to get home to my tea. My mum would half kill me if she knew I was here.'

Oh well, plenty of time.

'I'll be seeing you again?'

'Could be,' she conceded airily. 'Thought I might come along to the camp site later on; have a look at this posh caravan of yours.'

Damn! A spot of quick thinking was called for.

'That would have been great —'

'What d'you mean — would have been?' The voice had turned sharp, shrewish. 'Don't you want me to come, then?'

'Of course I do, Tracey.' He hit his brow with the flat of his hand in an attitude of despair. 'It's just that I've already promised to go fishing with a couple of lads from one of the other caravans.'

'You can put them off, can't you?'

'There's nothing I'd like better, honestly. But they're back off to the smoke in the morning and neither of them can handle a boat. I'm going to be here for another week.'

She mulled this over; pouted. 'Please yourself.'

He ran a finger down her cheek.

'But I'm not doing anything tomorrow.'

'I'll think about it.' Adrian fastened his lips to hers just to help her in her thinking. When she came up for air she turned her head, listening, and pushed him back.

'Listen!'

He stayed where he was as she ducked back down, aware of the sound of an oncoming car.

'I thought you said no traffic ever used this track?'

'Neither it does. It only goes to Pendrufford Point. Must be some idiot tourist, and we'll have to wait for them to turn round and come back.' Tracey was fretting with anxiety. 'It'll take them ages with all those potholes.'

'Surely we can make a run for it once they've passed?'

'I wouldn't dare.' Her distress was piteous. 'If anyone was to see me and my mum got to hear about it, she'd skin me alive.'

They cowered down together, just like the bloody babes in the wood, thought Adrian. He felt ridiculous. Directly the car had passed, grinding along in second gear, he raised his head.

'It was a red one —'

'Must have been Malcolm. He's ever so late, though.'

'Malcolm?'

'He drives the post office van. That means we're stuck here till he comes back. He's the biggest gossip out. If he sees us, it will be all over the village by tonight.'

Some of her tension was communicating itself to Adrian. His eyes narrowed.

'It wasn't a post office van. It was a small red Fiat.'

Relief eased from the girl like air from a balloon.

'One of those little tiny ones with a sunroof?' He nodded. 'That's all right then. It won't be coming back.'

He grasped her by the arm. 'Whose car is it, Tracey?'

'Get off, you're hurting me! It's all right, I tell you. We can go now. It won't be coming back.'

'Whose car is it?'

'What's it to you whose car it is? The people who bought Pendrufford have a car like that. Must have come down early or something.'

It was just before six when Chris called out an unfeeling good night to Hugh, still struggling away trying to balance his register totals. He entered the deserted office and picked up the phone. Still no reply. Beginning to simmer with resentment and anger he headed for the car park.

Sitting quietly on the grass beside his car was a familiar figure.

'Maria?'

'Yes, sir. My mother said I wasn't to come back, but I did rather want to talk to you. Do you mind?'

He glanced quickly round at the blank school windows,

the deserted playground; surprised how pleased he was to see her.

'No, not a bit. I'm glad. Jump in. Let's go somewhere quiet.'

The track down to Pendrufford Point was narrow and twisting and unmetalled. It bumped its way between high hedges of earth and stone which, even in the heat, were moist and green with damp fern and ivy and bramble. On the left were cultivated fields belonging to the farm; to the right, through rough and barren land, would lie the sea.

Caroline was tired and happy. She had taken her time on the journey, stopping for a pub lunch near Stonehenge, a cream tea at a Devon farmhouse. Now she felt refreshed and good, all her old confidence restored.

She felt the usual tremor of excitement as she approached the headland at snail's pace. It was some half-mile from the village as the crow flew, yet the house was tucked away round a corner, completely out of sight. With any luck at all, no one would know she had arrived.

Which was just as she had wanted it. Tomorrow she would be ready to meet them all,- prepared in her mind for everything she had planned to do. Tonight the only thing she wanted was to speak with Chris, and set his mind at rest. Poor dear, he must be sick with worry, but everything would be just fine once she explained how she had come ahead early to the place they loved so much, to get their home all ready for the long weeks of summer.

That was it. Phone Chris.

Phone! Mother! Oh dear God! She'd forgotten all about phoning her from a wayside garage. Poor Mother, sitting waiting for her with a meal lovingly prepared! She'd do that first; then Chris; then an early night with no telltale lights in the windows to carry across the bay to watching eyes from the village shore.

The car bucked as it emerged from the unfrequented lane on to the shelf of land where the small house lay hidden from view by scrub and woodland. She drew up and stopped; climbed out and flexed her cramped limbs, breathing in again the familiar smell of seaweed and brine.

The front door stood open. Caroline frowned.

She walked forward slowly; peered in at the open doorway.

'Hello? Anybody home?'

There was a scuffle of movement and a figure came out from the kitchen into the shadowed hall.

Caroline's eyes widened, first in surprise, then in recognition, and finally in terror as a pair of hands reached out and grasped her firmly by the throat.

CHAPTER 3. SATURDAY

By midnight the moon was full and high over Chandlers Grove. Dark and deserted, it had taken on a ghostly charm with homes and trees silhouetted black against the sky.

Chris coasted to the kerbside. No lights anywhere, but few of his neighbours stayed up long after the late night news. Nor, it appeared, was Caroline sitting up wondering where he was, knowing in her turn some of the anxiety which had haunted him all day.

Their bedroom was at the back of the house. She might well be lying there, wide awake and worried. Well, so be it. It would do no harm for once to establish that she did not have a monopoly on inconsiderate behaviour. And if she wanted to make a great scene, he could cope with that as well. Caroline always claimed that she was a great believer in clearing the air; this time, Chris was perfectly prepared to agree with her.

He'd had enough of the unspoken undercurrents and implications which had baffled him on Thursday. He had thought of little else all day, and especially over the last couple of hours. He did not care whether she were asleep or not. Tonight, they were going to talk.

He released the seat-belt, climbed out and made a vain attempt to close the car door quietly. Chandlers Grove was a respectable neighbourhood. He tiptoed up the garden path to the front door.

The hollow ring which emanates from empty houses sent out its message even before his key was in the latch. Indoors, his movements echoed strangely off the walls. He went from room to room, a slow malignant anger building up inside him.

And then the phone rang: shrill and demanding.

'Hello? Christopher Quinn here.'

The silence was eerie, insulting.

Chris replaced the receiver thoughtfully. It was not unheard of for disaffected pupils to phone their teachers late at night with obscenities or heavy breathing. He had never had such a call himself; it was usually the female staff who suffered — women living alone.

He stood by the phone, then took off the receiver and placed it on the Adam table.

At Pendrufford Point the moonlight fell in a shower of silver on wrinkled seas. Trees, boats and headland stood sharply etched against a luminous sky. From a clump of elms an owl called and swooped past on silent wings.

Adrian caught his breath. He had never known such stillness. And all those stars: blue-rinsed points of light embedded in a blanket of purple velvet. For the first time he began to understand why Susanne had chosen to bury herself at the back of beyond. Stan too. Affluent dropouts, that's what they were. He didn't blame them really.

His dad always said to get out when the going was good, to quit when you're winning. Never had a chance to do it himself, poor devil, dying like that. He'd have been proud of his son, if he could see him now. Chip off the old block, people said. Bright, ambitious, eager to learn. Doing well too, for a youngster. He enjoyed it all, the planning and the excitement. Being self-employed was the only life worth living.

He felt an unexpected sense of well-being. Funny thing, happiness. You could never count on it. The only thing you could ever count on was enjoyment: enjoyment of success and money, of girls and admiration, of freedom to order your own existence. He'd really enjoyed himself tonight.

Adrian picked up his fishing gear, tucked his black oilskins under his arm and ran lightly up the rocks. Time to get back to the caravan; get some sleep.

Before the small house he stopped, staring thoughtfully at its blank sightless windows. He shook his head, shrugged. Not to worry. It had been a terrific evening.

Chris could hear a distant hammering. It intruded its intermittent thumping into his fuddled brain with an insistence which dragged him through the borders of consciousness.

Twice he broke the surface of sleep before recognizing that he had a visitor who did not intend to go away.

Eight o'clock; eight o'clock on a Saturday morning. And someone was beating the door down. The milkman, of course: a sour individual with jaundiced views on his clients' credit rating.

Chris threw back the bedclothes and struggled into a navy bathrobe, grabbing his wallet from chest of drawers. Barefoot and heavy-lidded with sleep, he padded through to the hall; opened the door.

On the step, a smiling policeman: massive-shouldered and moustached. One of the older generation of beat bobbies now deployed in keeping order from the obscurity of a car parked outside.

'Good morning sir. Police Constable Purvis. Sorry to trouble you at this hour.'

'Not at all.' Chris smoothed back his hair. 'What can I do for you?' An awakening of memory. 'Nothing wrong with Maria, is there?'

'Mr Quinn? Mr Christopher Quinn?'

'That's right. Look, won't you come in?'

'Thank you very much, sir.' The officer removed his cap, tucked it under his left arm, followed him into the sitting-room. His eyes lingered on the displaced telephone in the hall, and Chris put it back in position.

'This Maria, sir. That would not be your wife, now would it?' He had planted his feet firmly on the carpet.

'My wife?' The first tremor of fear. 'No, Maria is just a child — a pupil of mine who's been having a bad time lately.'

'I see, sir.'

Constable Purvis went in for long silences. Chris checked the impulse to ask him to sit down, wondered how he should address the man. Officer or Constable sounded ridiculous, Mr Purvis even more so, in the circumstances. What circumstances?

'We've had a call at the station. A lady called Mrs Marjorie Barrett.'

'That's Caroline's mother! Nothing's happened to my wife, has it?'

'That is what Mrs Barrett was wondering, sir. When your wife still hadn't turned up late last night, she and her husband became rather concerned. You know how it is, sir.' His smile contained a hint of apology. 'It seems that every time they phoned this number they either got the engaged signal or there was no reply. She'd read stories about people lying unconscious from gas fumes and suchlike, and not discovered for days. Asked us if we'd just come round and check that all was well.'

So that was where Caroline had gone! Back to Bourne-mouth. That she hadn't arrived when expected did not come as a great surprise. She'd probably had a puncture, or a breakdown; spent the night at the nearest hotel. Still, she should have phoned her parents. She was inclined to take them very much for granted.

'I expect Mrs Quinn just delayed her trip, did she, sir? Left early this morning, perhaps?'

Chris reacted to the prompting with a smile. No one was more likely to resent any enquiry into her movements than Caroline.

'I don't really know. My wife has been visiting a friend, and I'm not too clear about her immediate plans. But it's very likely that she is on her way to Bournemouth now. We always spend the summer in Cornwall, and she likes to see something of her family as well. I'm fairly tied up with work in the last week of term.'

Why did he feel he was telling Constable Purvis much more than he wanted to know?

'Quite so, sir. No doubt you're right, and your wife will be in touch very soon.'

'I'm sure of it. She'll be appalled to have caused you all this trouble.'

'Very proper, sir. If you could just let me have the name and address of this friend your wife's been staying with?'

Chris stroked his chin. Best to be frank.

'I'm afraid I don't know it. I know the woman's called Helen, but I've never met her. My wife met her at some Adult Education class — floristry, I think.' He thrust his hands deep into the pockets of his bathrobe. 'You don't think she's in any sort of trouble, do you?'

'I shouldn't think so for a moment, sir. But if Mrs Quinn doesn't get in touch soon, either with you or with her parents, it might be a good idea to check with this woman. We could probably trace her through the education people.'

Now he knew exactly how a parent must feel when a much-loved child had strayed: torn between shocked anxiety and rage.

'But as you say, sir, she'll probably turn up safe and sound and wondering what all the fuss was about. It's our job to check out enquiries, Mr Quinn.'

'Of course!'

The atmosphere was more relaxed, almost friendly.

'Do you get many enquiries like this?'

'You'd be surprised. Around three thousand people go missing—really missing—every year. And about half of those are never traced.'

Chris stood very still. 'Good Lord! I'd no idea. Whatever happens to them all?'

The massive shoulders shrugged. 'What indeed, sir?' He withdrew his cap from under his arm. 'No doubt you'll be good enough to ring us at the station as soon as you, or your mother-in-law, hear from your wife?'

'I will indeed.'

Chris led the way to the front door and opened it.

The police officer nodded towards the grey Volkswagen outside.

'Your car, sir? I take it Mrs Quinn has a car of her own?'

'Yes.' He hesitated. 'Would you like its description, registration number?'

'Why not, sir?' He noted the details in his notebook. 'You didn't think to use the garage last night, Mr Quinn, your wife being away?'

'It never occurred to me. Force of habit, I expect. Caroline—my wife's car is a fairly new acquisition and she keeps it beautifully. I always park mine in the road.'

'Very natural, sir. We'll look forward to hearing from you then, Mr Quinn. Good morning.'

As he switched the kettle on, Chris realized that he had become very angry. Thanks to Caroline, he had just experienced as awkward and humiliating an interview as he could remember.

Another knock at the door.

This time he flung it open.

Police Constable Purvis.

'Sorry to trouble you again, sir, but I wonder if I might take a quick look inside your garage?'

A finger of apprehension prickled down his spine.

'Why?' His voice was testy. 'Do you expect to find my wife tied up in a paper parcel or something?'

'Now there's no need to take that attitude, sir. I'm only doing my job.'

'Yes of course. I'm sorry. Help yourself.'

'You don't keep it locked at night?'

Chris tried to laugh. 'I can't win, can I? No, we don't always lock it, I'm afraid. I know we should.'

'You would if you knew how much car theft there was.'

'Yes, you're right of course. I promise I'll keep it locked in future. And I'm sorry if I was rude just now.'

'Think nothing of it, Mr Quinn.' Constable Purvis treated him to a fatherly smile. 'Can't be very pleasant having a bobby on your doorstep asking questions. Very understandable. We never take it as personal.'

Pulling his belt closer, Chris led the way round to the side of the house, released the handle of the grey metal door.

Apart from the lawn-mower and other garden tools, the garage was empty.

Tracey's Saturday job at Susanne's was supposed to start at nine; but now that she'd been given her own key, her time-keeping had grown a little elastic. She switched on the lights to flood the salon with fluorescent daylight glow. Ever so nice it looked, much better than it did before Mrs Hyson bought the business. Much easier to clean too.

The walls were white-painted, and the woodwork picked out in palest coffee cream. The primrose porcelain basins were reflected in shining chrome, the soft padded seating a cheerful tan. Lots of plants on shelves and floor, really pretty. Tracey thought the whole effect was lovely, but then, whatever she might think of Mrs Hyson, she certainly had taste.

Tracey slipped off her jacket—black with scarlet piping—and hung it from the coat-rack. Took from its pocket two small plastic bottles and unscrewed their caps: one green, the other, red. Holding them over one of the basins, she filled the first with pink shampoo, the second with hair conditioner from the large containers on one of the shelves, screwed the caps back on, wiped them with tissue, and returned them to her jacket pocket.

In the right-hand drawer beneath the counter she found the latest delivery of lipsticks, selected one and drew a line with care on the inside of her wrist. Head to one side, she examined the colour and rejected it. In the left-hand drawer Susanne kept her box of samples of exotic perfumes: some eighteen tiny phials in fitted grooves. Tracey had been working her way through them week by week.

With immense care she prised off one of the plastic tops and withdrew the wand attached to it. Stroked it along her other wrist and waited for her body warmth to release the scent.

It smelt gorgeous, simply gorgeous.

She sighed and replaced the phial. It must be wonderful to be able to afford the very best of everything: perfume, make-up, clothes. To be able to look like Mrs Hyson, who wasn't really pretty when you came to look at her, but always managed to look so stylish. She knew it, too.

Better get on with the job if she was going to meet Adrian after her dinner. She eyed the net curtains; they looked perfectly crisp and fresh. No need to do them again this week. So did the windows. Perhaps just a wipe-over with a duster and a damp cloth along the sill where small dead flies tended to collect.

The dusting became transformed into a vigorous polishing movement as she caught sight of Susanne coming along the road. By the time she pushed open the door Tracey was panting heavily with exertion.

'Hello, Mrs Hyson. Come down to check I'm doing the job properly, have you?'

Susanne's eyebrows lifted slightly. 'Why—do you think that I ought to?'

'Well, that's a nice thing to say.'

Susanne laughed and walked round behind the counter.

'It was you who put the idea into my head.' She opened the left-hand drawer and sniffed the air with interest. Tracey felt her palms growing damp.

'I was only joking, Mrs Hyson. You don't usually come down to the shop on Saturdays.'

'I just popped in to pick up one of those perfume samples that arrived last week. It's ruinously expensive but I think it's terrific.' She picked out one of the phials, held it up and smiled. Not a particularly friendly smile either. 'I see you approve of it too.'

A dull red flush crept up Tracey's face. She never knew quite how to take Mrs Hyson. She gave a sullen jerk of the shoulders.

'I was just taking a look at them' She breathed heavily on the glass and rubbed the mist away.

'Of course. After all, they are samples. We get them so that customers can try them out. When you leave school and start a job, I shall expect you to be one of my best customers.'

'Oh yes, Mrs Hyson.'

'Good.'

Tracey was not quite sure whether Mrs Hyson meant what she said, or whether she was telling her in a round-about way that she knew the girl was engaged in petty pilfering.

'I'm going to borrow it myself, just for this evening.'

Tracey shot her a knowing smile. 'One of the perks of the job, Mrs Hyson?'

Susanne's lips folded together. 'I suppose you could say that.' Her voice had turned chilly. 'You won't forget to take down the curtains, will you? You can rinse them through while the floor is drying.'

'Of course, Mrs Hyson. You going somewhere special tonight then?'

'Only to Melanie's—Mrs Quinn's. An old friend of Alex's has come down and we're all going over for drinks this evening. Nothing very grand.'

'Oh yes? Many of you going?'

'Just the two of us, and Alex, and Geoff Taverner, of course.'

Tracey looked up from her work.

'Won't Mr and Mrs Quinn be going too?'

'Of course they will. They're giving the party. I must be off, Tracey. Goodbye.'

Tracey watched her leave, one hand clutching the polishing cloth, the fingers of the other stroking backward and forward along her lower lip as she pondered over the significance of that remark. Why weren't the Pendrufford Quinns going too?

Something very odd was going on.

'How do I look?' Alexis Quinn spun round to show off her full-skirted dress of candy-striped pink.

Toby, who had also taken some care with his appearance in honour of Melanie's party, stood back and adjusted his glasses.

'Virginal.'

'Thank you.' The left-hand dimple he had forgotten all about came and went.

'Clean and scrubbed and wholesome.'

'Like a baked potato?'

Toby laughed. 'You look terrific. Well worth the wait. Do you realize I've spent two long days dampening down my ardour and touring round Cornwall inspecting ancient forts and tumuli and derelict engine-houses on your account?'

'That was Melanie. She's a great one for the social niceties and she will go organizing everybody, including me if she gets half a chance. This is her first attempt at social eventing since they moved up to Mafia Mews. It will give her a chance to see if she approves of you or not.'

'Good God! Third degree stuff, do you mean?'

'Just a bit. All very tactful, of course. Melanie believes that it is right to take a real personal interest in people she meets. Not out of inquisitiveness; she really is interested.'

Toby fingered his tie. 'Couldn't we just slope off and have a quiet drink instead?'

'No, we couldn't. She'd be terribly upset. She's probably gone to a lot of trouble. Anyhow, she's bound to approve of you — clean-cut, ambitious young man with a steady job and excellent prospects. Just like Russell was at your age. It's people like Chris and me she worries about who don't have any ambitions at all.' Her brow crinkled. 'Wasn't it you who always wanted to be a policeman?'

He gave an embarrassed shrug. 'When I was a boy, yes. But they don't go in for myopic policemen nowadays. Imagine you remembering that. What about you? You'd no idea what you were going to do in the old days.'

'Still haven't. Deplorable, isn't it? I did manage to get a degree, but then Daddy died and it's been pretty hectic ever since. We had to sell up Goldenacre for a start, and

I've spent a lot of time doing this place up. Might go in for bed and breakfast, or invest in some more dinghies and rent them out, or something.'

'You're joking.'

'No, I'm not. I don't want to leave Treskellan and there's not a lot of scope for lotus-eating graduates down here. Don't you just love Shrimp Cottage?'

She looked round, pride of possession shining in her eyes. The room was low and beamed with dark wood, its walls of solid granite, some three foot thick, the stonework emulsioned over in white. Two original small rooms had been knocked into one: the sitting area furnished in pine and carpeted in rust. Yellow curtains at small sash windows, furniture upholstered in cheerful chintz; a huge granite fireplace stacked with logs; on the walls, gleaming brass and copper. The kitchen area was small and bright, tiled in sandstone, its stable door open on to the garden.

'I like it. All except the name. Whatever made you call it Shrimp Cottage?'

'I didn't. It's always been called Shrimp Cottage and one doesn't break with tradition down here. There are two tiny bedrooms upstairs—' she waved at the open steps which divided the room— 'and I've had a microscopic bathroom built out at the back with a real bath. Come and see the garden.'

She held out her hand and led him out on to a patch of grass which disappeared into a stretch of undergrowth leading down to a small stream which ran alongside the cottage.

'I've still got a lot to do out here, but that stream is the same one we played in at Goldenacre when we were children.' She pointed up the steeply rising hill. 'It's up there, behind the trees. I knew I wouldn't mind moving out too much if I could still have that stream in my garden. You can lie in bed and listen to it, just like we used to. Especially in the winter, when it's really rushing past.'

If there had been the suggestion of a quiver in her voice, it had been taken in hand very quickly. Toby searched around for a more cheerful topic.

'It's a super little house. Next year I'll come down and be your first bed-and-breakfast guest. If you'll have me.'

'Of course. I rather fancy myself as a seaside landlady. What on earth's keeping Geoff?'

'Geoff?' Toby was annoyed. He'd heard the name before. Mrs Quinn had used it on the phone, implying an intimacy with Alex he hadn't cared for.

'Yes. He's coming too. He's in the holiday let next door. Been coming down here for years and years.'

'Oh.' Toby was not pleased. 'What does he do, this Geoff?'

Alex perched on the low stone wall and sighed.

'My God, you still do it! Try to classify people by the jobs they do so that you can make prejudgments about their incomes and family backgrounds and all those idiotic things that don't matter a scrap.'

'All right, all right, I only asked.' Alex always had been argumentative.

'If you really want to know what Geoff does, I'll tell you. Fifty weeks of the year he gets home from work, cooks himself a meal and drives twelve miles to hospital to visit his wife. Then he drives back and watches the box and goes to bed. Weekends too. Once a year Sheila's parents take over and he comes down here just like they used to before the accident.'

'I'm sorry. Car accident?'

'Yes. Five years ago. She was so badly brain-damaged it's doubtful if she even recognizes him. As he was driving at the time, he's got just about all the guilt he can handle, so he's not always the most charming of men. Spends most of his life punishing himself as he can't find anyone else to do it for him, in the hope that he'll feel better. It doesn't seem to work.'

'Poor devil.'

'Yes. He's also quite a gifted amateur photographer; Sheila was something of an artist too. I'm not too sure about his actual job; I know he works in a bank up in the Midlands somewhere.'

The Meadowbank Estate had been gouged out of the hillside with a ferocity which beggared description. Toby stood appalled at the scale of devastation which had been visited on one of the most beautiful sites in the county.

'I just don't believe it! How could anyone in their senses have let it happen?'

Across a stretch of hard-baked mud was scattered a confetti of whitewashed boxes with neither charm nor character: each house separated from its neighbour by plastic chain drooping from concrete pillars. Most had double garages, many had huge pits dug in the garden promising a rash of swimming pools to come. Only a few showed signs of habitation—half-erected larchwood fencing, garden loungers straight from Harrods.

Geoff Taverner, square and stocky, with a pleasantly ugly, broad face, gave a short laugh.

'The man has taste, Alex. He doesn't care too much for our prestigious abomination.'

'You mean people actually want to buy houses like this?' Toby remembered too late that Alex's brother had already done just that.

'Oh yes,' said Alex. 'Not many local people, of course. They're mostly second homes for the affluent yachting types from up country. Next week they'll be swarming all over the place, complete with boats and surfboards and children. Arrogant lot, most of them. They foregather in the Green Dragon every lunch-time, talking in loud voices and calling the landlord squire.'

'He must love that.'

'So long as they go on spending money, he puts up with

being patronized quite cheerfully,' said Geoff. 'The only permanent residents are retired people who expect to enjoy a happy retirement by the sea, poor fools. They tend to shrivel up and die of utter loneliness when the fine weather stops. Happens all the time.'

'Russell's place,' said Alex a shade defensively, 'is that one at the far end, backing on to Goldenacre. It's in quite the best position, with a fantastic view.'

Toby turned round to look back at the cragged coastline, the creaming surf, the scatter of yacht sails in the sun. The view was indeed magnificent, and as they drew near he could see that The Shrubberies would, one day, justify its name. A lot of work had already been carried out on the garden: turf newly laid and not yet settled; a host of young shrubs staked out to provide seclusion in the years to come.

Four people were already on the patio in front of the house where green and orange garden seats were grouped round a white circular table with a top like a paper doily. To one side was a huge matching umbrella fringed in white; one wide hammock seat, four padded deckchairs with footrests. Behind the group full length sliding windows framed in aluminium stood open on to a large through lounge, parquet floored, scattered with rugs. A table close to the window held bottles, glasses, dishes of nuts, olives, crisps.

The older woman coming towards them with outstretched arms just had to be Melanie Quinn. She reminded him of his first Akela when he'd joined the Cubs: angular, shapeless, a cotton skirt bunched round her waist, bare legs. Good big teeth and fine lines developing round the eyes, affectionate and caring. A high-pitched voice, a quick nervous smile.

Behind her came Russell, in fawn corduroy trousers and yellow pullover: a man used to authority, genial and friendly.

'We were all so glad you could come.' She really meant it too, thought Toby. Her pleasure was naked, almost frightening. He smoothed down his collar with that particular unease which attends a gathering whose declared objective is informality. 'You must meet our very good friends, Susanne and Stanley Hyson.'

He shook hands; so this was the girl he'd spoken to on the phone. Tall and slim, exquisitely groomed in a dress of green chiffon, honey blonde hair forming a curtain of silk falling to her shoulders. Her eyes were dancing, mischievous; he would like to get to know Susanne Hyson. Very much younger than her husband, though: a striking man with intelligent eyes and long tapering fingers, reserved and courteous. They made a handsome pair.

'I trust,' said Geoff quietly, 'that your intentions towards our Alex are quite honourable? Our hostess will soon discover if they aren't.'

Susanne Hyson smothered a giggle and turned away. Melanie waved him into a chair and sat beside him. Alex had vanished into the house with Russell.

'And how long are you staying in this part of the world, Mr Wilde? Or can we call you Toby?'

Toby avoided looking at the others.

'Of course. Only till tomorrow, I'm afraid. I'm touring around without any particular destination. I'll have had three nights at Port Laverock, and tomorrow I'll head off north towards Wales.'

'Oh that is a shame! And you've had to waste such a long time before seeing Alex. I really am terribly sorry; it was all my fault.'

Something warned Toby he was in for a very boring evening.

'Not at all. I've really enjoyed seeing all the sights down here. I've been to Land's End, and explored a lot of stone circles and dolmens and things. I've had a look at some of the mineshafts and engine-houses—I had no idea there were so many.'

He could sense Susanne's eyes beginning to glaze over. Geoff's fingers drummed quietly against the arm of his chair. Russell and Alex were pouring drinks and chatting together inside the open windows. Toby would have given a lot to have joined them.

'Oh yes,' Melanie was assuring him. 'Very dangerous, a lot of them. Completely unfenced, you know. Terribly dangerous when you think of all the people who come down here on holiday with children and dogs.'

Toby nodded gravely, and listened to the beginning of a dissertation on the history of mining in Cornwall in the nineteenth century. The discourse was happily discontinued with the arrival of drinks: glasses of wine, red, white and rosé, in glasses rimmed with silver gilt, engraved with snowdrops. Russell sat down next to his wife, offered Toby a cigarette from a leather case. He shook his head.

Melanie nodded approval.

'Oh I'm so glad you don't. I've done everything in my power to persuade Russell to give it up. Such an unpleasant habit and so dangerous to health. He's developed a very nasty little cough recently, and I'm sure all this smoking has something to do with it.' Toby felt he should apologize to Russell for exposing him to public reproach, except that it didn't seem to bother him in the least. 'Such a bad example for Angela too, at such an impressionable age.'

Alex looked round. 'Where *is* Angela?'

'She's having a bath, dear. Came home very hot and flushed and I thought it best. She'd been out riding with Penny and Gill.' She turned to include Toby in the exchange. 'They are two of her friends, very nice girls.'

Toby could think of no answer to this. He nodded with suitable gravity. Why was it that really nice ladies were often so incredibly boring?

'So you are a solicitor, Toby? That must be very interesting.'

'Actually,' said Alex, 'he's really a detective manqué.'
Melanie looked up, startled. 'He's a what?'
Russell flicked ash from his cigarette and laughed.
'Manqué means failed, dear. Alex is showing off.
Toby's not really a detective.'
'He always wanted to be one, though. Only took up the
law because he'd look silly in a helmet and hornrimmed
glasses.'
Geoff leant forward. 'Is that right? You're a criminal
lawyer?'
Toby glared at Alex. 'No, of course it isn't. I've only
been a solicitor for five minutes.'
He was just calculating how long it would before he
might with decency take his leave when a slip of a girl
came through the doorway: neat and dark, pleasant in
manner. The daughter of the house: Angela Quinn. She
shook hands with courtesy but no obvious enthusiasm.
'We can all go in and eat now,' announced Melanie.
'Just as soon as we've finished our drinks.' Toby's heart
sank. 'Nothing very special, I'm afraid. Just a cold buffet,
if that is all right.'
'That,' he said desperately, 'will be delightful.'
'Angela has had a very busy week,' she told him with
pride. 'She's been playing Titania in the school production of *A Midsummer Night's Dream*. She was very
good too. But I'm sure she must be very tired.'
Angela gave her mother a quick smile. 'You mustn't
fuss, Mummy. I'm fine, honestly. You're the one who's
looking tired, if you ask me.'
'Just the same, I want you to go to bed early tonight.'
Susanne turned her head, listening.
'Melanie, I think your phone's ringing.'
Russell jumped up and ran into the house. Melanie fell
silent while Susanne talked to Geoff. As Russell came
back out, she gave a sharp cry:
'Why—whatever is the matter?'

All heads turned. Russell was standing in the open doorway with a worried frown on his face. He reached into his pocket for a cigarette.

'That was Chris. Wondering if Caroline was down here.'

'Down here? Caroline? Why should she be down here?'

'He hasn't seen her since Thursday night when she went to stay with a girl-friend.'

'But that's—what?—two days ago. Wherever can she be?'

'He's very worried. Apparently she planned to go on to her parents at Bournemouth, but never arived.'

Geoff's hands were clenched. 'Has he been to the police?'

'Yes. She was reported missing this morning.'

'But what makes him think she might have come here?'

'He says her car is missing as well. I think he was just checking to see if she was with us. Caroline does tend to do things on impulse, we all know that.'

Where each of the men looked distinctly worried, Melanie recovered quickly. Her voice was brisk: 'Caroline will be all right, you'll see. Very capable girl. They could have had an argument or something, and she's gone off to sulk.'

'Argument?' demanded Alex hotly. 'Chris? He wouldn't even know how to begin. The nearest he ever comes to a display of anger is a quiet grinding of the teeth. I don't like this at all, Russell.'

Her brother sat down and inhaled deeply: blew out the smoke in a long, steady stream.

'Neither does Chris. The police have been asking him a lot of questions. He thinks they believe he knows more about what's happened to Caroline than he's admitting.'

In days to come, Toby would be able to recall at will precisely how everyone reacted at that moment; positions, actions, expressions; a tableau frozen in time. Stanley

Hyson exchanging a quick glance with Susanne, who moved directly to Alex's side, concerned, supportive. Alex staring at her brother in stony incomprehension. Russell himself trying hard to keep the shock from showing on his face; and Melanie looking up at him, willing him some of her own strength and common sense. Geoffrey scowling ferociously at the tips of his shoes. Angela sitting, thoughtful, on the grass at their feet.

It was her voice which splintered the silence.

'What exactly did Chris say, Daddy? I think I'm still a bit confused.'

Russell looked down at her with affection, ruffled her hair and began to talk more easily, as though telling her a story.

'Two nights ago — on Thursday, that would be — Caroline spent the night with a friend called Helen. She wasn't back when Chris got home from school on Friday, so he just thought she'd stayed on another night.'

'But didn't he phone up to find out?' objected Alex.

'That's the trouble. He'd never met this woman. Didn't even know where she lived.'

Alex tried to smile. 'That sounds like Caroline.'

'They've managed to find this Helen and she says Caroline left her place yesterday morning. Then it seems she phoned her mother and said she'd be going there for the weekend. On her own.'

'Without even telling Chris, you mean?'

'So it seems.'

'But surely he was worried?'

Toby watched the exchange between brother and sister, and was reminded of Wimbledon tournaments: all heads moving back and forth following the two contenders.

'Well, not really,' admitted Russell. 'Not at that stage. He had to work late at school, and he'd rung home several times, but there was never any reply. So he went off for a drive into the country, out to the Chilterns. Didn't get home until after midnight.'

'Chris did that?' asked Alex in shocked amazement. 'Are you saying he got home in the small hours of the morning, and when he found Caroline wasn't there, he just went to sleep? And didn't even report it till the morning? I simply don't believe it!'

Russell's face was grim. 'Neither do the police, apparently. It was they who knocked him up to ask if she were safe. Her mother had become anxious.'

'I shouldn't worry too much, Alex,' said Melanie kindly. 'They may well have some sort of tiff — a disagreement we don't know anything about. It's not the sort of thing Chris would be likely to tell anyone else, now is it?'

'But why,' asked Angela, 'didn't Caroline's mother phone Chris direct? Surely that would have been much easier.'

'It seems they had tried. But Chris had left the receiver off the hook.'

'Why on earth did he do that?'

'I've no idea, Angela. He probably hadn't replaced it properly.'

Melanie nodded. 'It's easy done. I've done it myself once or twice, when I've been dusting, you know. I expect she'll turn up safe and sound any minute now. She certainly hasn't been down here.'

Angela started to speak; stopped when Geoffrey addressed himself to Toby.

'You should be able to tell us. When people go missing like this, what's usually behind it?'

Toby disliked being at the centre of attention in this domestic fracas. Like the Hysons, he had planned to keep well out of any theorizing. He looked with longing at his empty glass.

'I'm not altogether sure that it would be helpful, at this stage—'

'Well, do you know the answer or don't you?'

Nettled, he glared back at Geoff; rose to the bait.

'There are so many reasons. Amnesia for one.' He allowed time for that to be considered. 'Or people running away from something they don't want to face, like debts, or their parents, or an unhappy marriage. That sort of thing.'

'You mean,' asked Angela with interest, 'that Caroline might have gone off with someone else?'

Too bright by half, that child.

'I'm not suggesting that for a moment. Just talking about people generally. Husbands do it too, you know. But from what you say, that sounds very unlikely.'

If he had hoped to reassure them, he was wrong.

'All right,' said Geoff, 'that rules out those people who want to disappear. What about the others?'

Russell reached for another cigarette; Melanie picked up his lighter from the table and lit it for him. Toby's eyes met Susanne's, and she gave him a small nod of encouragement.

'There are always accidents, especially in lonely places. Or abductions, kidnapping. Suicide, sometimes. In a tiny minority of cases, of course, it can be quite serious, but you must believe that there's usually some perfectly simple explanation.'

Angela stretched out her arms and sighed.

'Poor old Uncle Chris. No wonder the police want to know what he's been up to. They always suspect the husband first, don't they? And there are some very funny things about that story of his.'

Melanie's reaction was swift and terrible. She upbraided the girl with outraged anger, cast scorn on her passion for reading silly detective books and packed her off to bed that very minute.

An interesting child, thought Toby, as she walked back into the house. Still too young to sense the unspoken thoughts of disloyalty which had struck her elders, but old enough to respond to the challenge of a puzzle; quite intriguing for a bright girl like Angela. And Angela was quite a bright youngster. Her parting remark had been short and to the point:

'I can't think why you don't just phone up Pendrufford and see if she's there.'

Melanie clapped a hand to her mouth.

'Of course. Why didn't we think of it? I just thought Chris was wondering if she was here with us.' Russell was already on his feet. 'No, darling, don't phone. We'll take the car over and have a look for ourselves. Just in case.'

Susanne also stood up. 'I'm sure you'd like us to go home, Melanie. I'm so sorry you're all so worried, but I know it will all turn out all right. Call us at once if there's anything we can do.'

Toby looked at Alex, at Geoff, looking for some signal to tell him whether he should leave as well.

'I'm sorry, Toby, but I'm going with them,' said Alex.

'Oh no you're not!' Melanie was back in command. 'No one is going home. Alex will stay here with her guests. Give everyone another drink, dear. We shan't be long.'

Russell was already backing an estate car out of the garage, and Melanie got in beside him.

At the end of the evening, Geoff walked with Toby back' to the village car park.

'Not quite the evening we all expected,' he said abruptly. 'You didn't see a lot of Alex.'

Toby kicked out at a stone in the road.

'No. But it was natural they'd all be worried.'

'Yes. Very close family, that. I was thinking, if you're not in any hurry, you might like a chance of seeing Alex again. Away from Melanie, I mean. There's an empty

bedroom at my place. Bit primitive. Junk food a speciality.
For a day or so. You being a friend of Alex.'

His first reaction was to recoil from the very idea; his
second was—like Angela's—a reprehensible curiosity, a
desire to know how the story would end. If Caroline
Quinn was not at Pendrufford, as had been established,
he'd quite like to know what had happened to her.

He would also have a chance to see Alex again; on her
own.

'Well, it's good of you to offer. Just for a day or so.'

'Fine. Bit out of my depths, you understand. Fond of
Caroline. Chris too. Very nice people. Bring your stuff
over in the morning.'

CHAPTER 4. SUNDAY

Treskellan parish church sat, squat and placid, in a mossy
garden studded with grey memorials of slate and stone.
Her single bell sent out its pure and perky invitation each
Sunday morning, that all who would might worship within
her walls.

Outside the lych-gate the faithful would foregather in
their Sunday best to come together in little groups of
affability, to break away and then reform in a ritual
dance enshrined in custom, muted and restrained. Later
they would walk, in couples or in families, over the path
of granite chips to the great west door.

Russell walked with measured step behind his wife and
daughter: Melanie crunching her way in silk two-piece,
and Angela treading carefully in shoes with heels, uncertain
how to deal with gloves and bag. In the vestibule he held
the swing door open to let them pass through into the dim
interior before joining the group whose turn it was to offer
a smiling welcome along with prayer and hymn books to

every member of the congregation.

The majority of these were men; men of an older generation than those he had held so much in awe when he was a boy. There were few left of his own generation who came to church at all; fewer still prepared to serve on the parochial church council, and to regard the service as an honour.

Russell enjoyed this weekly duty, the greeting of friends and strangers, the handing over of books to those who no longer had their own: another innovation he deplored. He would try to commit the unknown faces to memory so that he might recognize them later, on the beach or in the pub. He knew that it pleased them enormously that he had remembered them; people enjoyed being recognized. It made them feel appreciated.

His father had been churchwarden for nearly forty years. One day, not long in coming, he would follow in that tradition, not only by natural inheritance but by fitness and devotion to duty. The present incumbent was not a local man: a retired naval officer whose wife had not long died. It was an ill-kept secret that he planned to join his brother soon at his home in Guernsey.

If all went well, Russell should fill his place. Perhaps the greatest challenge of his life, to follow so directly in his father's footsteps. He would never forget the day when Dr Quinn first realized that his elder son did not enjoy the natural academic gifts he had expected of his children. Russell himself had known it for many years, but had battled his way through primary school by stolid determination and hard work.

It was at a parents' evening just before his transfer to secondary schooling that Dr Quinn had heard his son damned with faint praise. The teacher was new to the school and strange to the ways of Treskellan. And she had been the first to face Dr Quinn with the truth: that Russell was reliable and hardworking but was never going to set the world on fire. Even less was he likely to enter the medical profession.

Clearly the woman was a fool. Consultations began: letters and phone calls; visits of inspection to private schools with proud and proven academic records. In September Russell left Treskellan for a boarding-school in Kent. Within a year he was back, but by then he had a new baby sister and his mother was dead. No more was heard of boarding-schools. Dr Quinn had decided that above all he would keep his family together, and no one tried to dissuade him.

Russell missed his mother badly. Where his father had been overwhelming and remote, she had been pretty and gentle. He built up in his memory an idealized picture of the woman who had laughed with him, encouraged him, and, far from resenting the baby girl who had taken her life, saw in her a sacred charge laid upon him. The care of Alex, and of Chris — three years his junior — he pursued with single-minded dedication: a responsibility he had carried out for twenty-three years.

Things became easier once he had Melanie to help him, to share his hopes and ambitions. There was no one quite like a loyal and loving wife, and no wife on earth more loyal and loving than Melanie. They both adored Angela. It would have been perfect if there had been a son as well, but that was not to be. He could not expect Melanie to go through all that again.

They had everything else: loving family and friends; a new home equipped just as Melanie had wanted; a decent income from his post as general manager of the largest departmental store in the district; status and position. Russell could now admit that he was happier as a big fish in his small and familiar pool than chasing after greater promotion and prospects in one of the big cities. His future, please God, would always be right here in Treskellan.

If only Caroline's disappearance were satisfactorily resolved, the omens for the future seemed excellent. He wondered how he might feel if Melanie had gone missing, and shuddered. Chris must be going through hell.

Inside the church with its familiar smell of mould and polish, Angela knelt beside her mother in the pew towards the rear of the nave where the Quinn family had always sat. The pews were hard and shiny, with a strip of maroon felt the only concession to comfort. She shuffled her knees on to one of the navy hassocks finely embroidered by Great-grandmother Quinn and felt her tights spring a ladder down one leg.

Propriety demanded that she bend her head, close her eyes for a few statutory moments out of respect rather than conviction. From behind her hands she could watch the sidesmen encouraging visitors into the front pews rather than let them cluster together at the back, but she could tell the regular worshippers directly by their assurance, their air of proprietorship. They knew their way around and intended to show it, unlike those for whom morning worship was a rare experience.

Angela had been confirmed at the age of twelve because it had seemed to be expected of her: something it was wise to have done, like innoculations, at a certain age. She had hoped for some great mystical revelation like Paul on his way to Damascus, but was not especially surprised that it didn't happen. What she did enjoy was the grand magnificence of church language, and she joined in the general thanksgiving that their reactionary vicar had resisted all pressure to chat up the Almighty in the current vernacular.

She sat back on the quilt of maroon felt; let her eyes rove as always over the dark handcarved pew ends, the splendid barrel roof, the plain glass windows and leafy branches waving outside, the massive and ancient stone font at which she had been baptized: the only grandchild

Dr Quinn was ever to see. The church had been crammed to the doors on the day of his funeral. Angela had felt tremendously important that day, with all eyes on the family in mourning. She'd tried to look young and frail and sad. In a weird sort of way she'd enjoyed being at the centre of the stage. She had been sorry he'd died, though. Caroline could be dead too, perhaps? But Caroline was not an old man, she was still quite young. Please God, make Caroline go back home to Uncle Chris. Today. If you do, I'll really try to believe in you.

A discreet disturbance: the organist making an entry, sheets of music in one hand. Any minute now he would begin the voluntary and the church bell would stop. A quiver of anticipation rustled round the church as when the lights in a theatre die away.

Russell strode with confidence and bowed head down the aisle, knelt briefly beside his wife. Together they rose, settled themselves; glanced round, exchanging restrained nods of acknowledgement with others in the congregation.

The organist slid into position along his seat; placed his music on the stand; flexed his shoulders, his fingers.

All over the country, Morning Prayer was about to begin.

Far out in the bay Toby listened to the church bell, resting on the oars of his dinghy. Then it gave a small hiccup and stopped, leaving an abyss of silence. He began to row gently, waves rippling under the bow, twin rows of tiny whirlpools forming from drops of water falling from the blades.

Once again he asked himself how in the world he had come to be in his present predicament. He was supposed to be relaxing on holiday from a job which entailed involvement in the problems and anxieties of total strangers: worried about contracts and completion dates, the raising of mortgages. The last thing he needed was another spell of agonizing over other people's troubles: least of all the missing sister-in-law of a one-time girl-friend.

In the cold dawn of reason, which arrived rather late in the day, he could see his impulsive acceptance of Geoff Taverner's invitation of the night before as being one of the most stupid of over-reactions he could imagine. A day or two in the company of Alex would have been attractive in normal circumstances, but circumstances in the Quinn family were clearly far from normal. So they were a close, affectionate bunch of people, but the tension of the previous evening had seemed out of all proportion to the event. No one had been at all surprised that Russell had found no trace of Caroline at Pendrufford although it seemed that everyone had hoped fervently that she might be there.

The alternatives were too uncomfortable to contemplate; including the unspoken thought that Caroline might not be the faithful, loving wife they'd all supposed.

Toby had breakfasted early, determined to renege on his promise to Geoff if he possibly could. Quite what had happened to that resolution he was not quite sure. Its disappearance had something to do with the soft smudges under Alex's eyes, the pleasure on her face when he called at Shrimp Cottage to make his apologies.

Geoffrey too was glad to see him. He'd taken the suitcase from his car and shoved a mug of coffee in his hand while he was still searching for the words to explain his change of heart. And that was strange. Why should an unsociable chap like Geoffrey Taverner invite a man he barely knew to share his precious holiday?

From out in the bay Toby had a perfect view of the westward-facing village and beyond, from the large headland to the north round to the smaller arm of rock at Pendrufford Point. The original hamlet clustered closely round the harbour, while inland lay sporadic outbreaks of high density retirement bungalows grouped like small white Monopoly pieces.

Behind the sand dunes lay the golf-course, and beyond it he could glimpse some caravans hidden among the trees. But the finest site was that of Goldenacre, mercifully screened from the monstrosity known as the Meadowbank Estate, a gaping wound close to the village heart, a monument to tasteless affluence. He could see Alexis in the garden of The Shrubberies, keeping guard on the phone while the family was at church. Just in case, she had said with an apologetic laugh, Chris might call them up with some news.

Toby felt trapped. Even now Geoff was preparing Sunday lunch, having refused his offer of help. Get unpacked, he'd said. Take the boat out, have a look around. Come back when you feel like it.

Too early to go back yet. He glanced over his shoulder. Plenty of time to have a look at the house beyond Pendrufford Point. The one that Christopher Quinn had bought.

The sun was hot on his back as he sculled around the headland. The water was deep and clear, full of slabs of rock freckled in barnacles, fronded with trailing seaweed, green and brown.

On the far side a small stone house was tucked away, bathed in sunshine. The house that every child has drawn: a roof with chimneys, four windows, a door in the middle. There was a shelf of land in front, an outbuilding to one side, a wooden jetty straggling out over the rocks. It was enchanting.

Toby was seized by a rare pang of envy. Pendrufford was the country cottage of every townsman's dreams: dilapidated, secluded, swamped in honeysuckle and roses, with the sea surging yards from its door.

He pulled alongside the crumbling jetty, tied the painter to a rotting post, jumped ashore and crossed the grassy forecourt to the house. He pushed back purple and scarlet fuchsia from the window and looked inside.

The furnishings were not impressive. Like the holiday cottage Geoff was renting, they were strictly functional. But with time and care and money, all that would change. He moved to the second window; wondered how much the place had cost.

'Were you looking for someone?'

Toby spun round. A youth in his early twenties stood watching him, hands on hips, a touch of arrogance in his stance.

'No. I'm afraid I was just curious.' He felt embarrassed.

'You live here? In the village?'

There was something abrasive about his tone.

'Me — good Lord no. I'm on holiday. Look, I wasn't looking through those windows with any felonious intent, if that's what you think. The people who own this place are related to some friends of mine.'

'So they won't mind you snooping through their windows?'

Toby's right fist began to clench. 'I bet you made a lovely prefect when you were at school,' he said pleasantly.

The boy went on looking at him. Toby turned on his heel and walked with dignity back to the jetty, climbed back into the boat and cast off. When he caught his last glimpse of the cottage the boy was still standing there, looking after him.

Toby was still smarting at the memory as he pushed open Geoffrey's front door. Alex was sitting on the window-seat while Geoff ladled great dollops of stew on to heavy plates. It smelt a good deal better than it looked.

'Did I time it right?'

'We saw you coming,' said Alex. 'Time doesn't count for much down here. Strong Celtic influence. So long as we're in the right week, everything's fine.'

'It drives people mad when they first come down here,' Geoff confirmed. 'They actually expect tradesmen to turn up on time, and complete work on schedule. Silly. All that rushing around. Where does it get you?'

Toby could think of no answer to that, so he took his place at the table. Alex sat down facing him.

'Melanie was wondering if we'd like to go up to her place for dinner tonight.' Toby saw his own reaction mirrored on Geoff's face. 'I told her no, of course. She looks quite shattered, and she's not even family.'

'That figures.' Geoffrey sat down, picked up a knife and fork. 'She always goes through hell when her loved ones are suffering. Remember when Angela had her appendix out? The brisk efficiency thing is just a front. No news, then?'

'Not yet. I rang Chris just as soon as they'd gone to church. Much better than getting reports at second hand. He's off to Bournemouth today. He's quite convinced that the car's broken down and Caroline has put up at some hotel or something. Will check on them, and at garages, on the way. And if there's still no news, he thinks it right he should visit the old people. I do wish —' she stirred her fork aimlessly round her plate — 'she'd get in touch soon.'

'I'd like to think,' said Geoff with some venom, 'that Chris gives her a piece of his mind when she does. Worrying everybody sick like this.'

'Yes. If only we knew whether to be furious with her, or whether we really should be getting worried. It would make it much easier.'

Toby glanced from one to the other. Played with the idea of talking of happier things; changed his mind.

'You don't think it's a possibility that Caroline may have gone off for the weekend with someone else?'

'Caroline! Not for a moment. I've never seen two people so besotted with each other after seven weeks of married life, never mind seven years. That's right, isn't it, Geoff?'

Geoff looked as though she might be overstating the case, but nodded agreement. 'You think that's the likeliest answer, do you?'

'It's certainly the most common reason for a married woman to disappear. I'm sorry, Alex, but it's true. They run away with someone else.'

'You don't know Caroline.'

'Exactly,' said Geoff. 'The impartial viewpoint. Perhaps it's what we need.'

'You see, Alex, if she has, there might be a letter in the morning. It's easier to write than to telephone; no chance of arguments.'

She thought this over. 'At least we'd know something definite,' she admitted. 'But I'm sure you're wrong. Will the London police have notified the police down here as well, do you think?'

'Could be. I'm not too sure how much they bother with grown-up women who disappear for a day or two. Not a lot, I should think, provided there's no suspicion of foul—'

'Have some more stew,' said Geoff, too late to catch the conversational brick which thudded at his feet.

Toby accepted thankfully, grateful for the diversion.

'When you two have quite finished,' Alex interrupted, 'can we get back to the point?'

'Oh, give it a rest, Alex. Toby doesn't want to hear us chuntering away about Caroline all through lunch. He's told you: the great majority of people who go missing turn up safe and sound in a very short while. Now let's talk about something else.'

Alex's voice was small and stiff. 'Sorry if you find the subject boring. All I meant was that we've got to accept that something awful could have happened to her.'

'It is remotely possible—' Toby picked his words with care— 'that she may have come to some harm. Yes.'

Geoff snorted. 'Very delicately expressed; must be

great to have a legal mind, trained in doublespeak. You must give me some hints on how to call unpleasant things by pleasing-sounding names.'

Toby allowed wistful thoughts of Welsh mountains to flit across his mind.

Geoff picked up his plate and took it over to the sink. Crashed it into a basin already stacked with dirty dishes.

'All right, Alex. Let's go right over the top and get it over with. Caroline may be held captive by some band of brigands, or have committed suicide, or be lying in some remote spot with terrible injuries, or drowned at the bottom of some quarry. Or she may have been murdered by some roving maniac or come to some other sort of sticky end. Now are you satisfied?'

Toby studied his fingernails. Tomorrow he would pack his bag and leave, no matter what. He'd had enough. But Alex was smiling.

'Thanks, Geoff,' she said, 'I knew I could rely on you. To say it, I mean. That Caroline might be dead. But who—' she ran her finger along the tablecloth— 'would want to murder Caroline?'

It was after seven when Chris arrived back from Bournemouth. The flat was hot and airless. He went from room to room opening windows, steeling himself to find Caroline in none of them. He could not face another expectation dashed.

He rinsed out the dishes left in the sink; put an empty milk bottle on the step. Wandered through to the sitting-room, poured himself a scotch; set it down untasted on the mantelpiece. Sighed and stretched; rubbed at the fine layer of grit forming behind his eyelids. Looked around restlessly for something else to do, some physical activity which might disperse the explosive reserves of energy seeking for an outlet.

Activity, he thought wryly, had no connection with

achievement. For two days now he had been constantly on the move, enquiring, searching, visiting; friends, acquaintances and even strangers, both here and on the road to Bournemouth. And had achieved nothing. Time now to be still; to think and to order his thoughts.

The first was that nothing so far had indicated that Caroline had come to any harm. But, if she were safe, where in the world was she? Had she disappeared from choice or from coercion? As coercion seemed most unlikely, she must have vanished of her own free will; and whatever reason lay behind it, at least she would be safe, somewhere.

Most important, it seemed, was that very reason. If only he could identify that, he would be half way to finding her.

The only indication seemed to lie in her determination not to go to Treskellan for the summer. The more Chris tried to recall Caroline's exact behaviour on Thursday — and he had thought of little else — the more he became convinced that it had been both premeditated and untypical. Her apparent anger had carried a ring of insincerity, as though deliberately contrived. There had been no familiar outburst of sudden fury, swiftly over. When she had spoken of Treskellan and his family she had been calm and quiet; intent, it seemed, on giving pain. He might almost have thought she was afraid of going down to Cornwall; afraid to tell him the reason why. That was difficult to believe. Unless there were another explanation.

There was: the one he didn't want to think about; the one the police, out of long experience, had clearly favoured. The solution of the eternal triangle. Was it possible that there was another man in Caroline's life? It happened all the time these days, it seemed. I shouldn't worry too much, sir, they'd said. At the same time — and the words hovered unspoken in the air — we'll just bear in mind that you may have done her in. Sir.

Caroline's parents were clinging fiercely to the belief that she was safe and well. A wilful girl, they'd said, always had been; a girl of spirit and independence. Probably gone off on her own for a day or two to think something out. Perhaps there might have been some little disagreement between them, her mother had enquired, probing with genteel good manners, naked terror shining in swollen eyes.

The doorbell rang.

Police Constable Purvis.

'Good evening, sir.' As amiable and bland as ever; only his glance was a shade more searching. 'We've found your wife's car, Mr Quinn.'

Relief; delight; a dawning fear.

'Been reported found abandoned in a back street in Paddington. Thought you might like to come down to the station and have a chat with our CID lads.'

Tracey's eyes widened in pleased surprise at her first sight of Adrian's holiday caravan.

'It's ever so big, isn't it? For one person all by themselves, I mean.'

'I like being comfortable. Anyhow, I didn't plan on being all by myself all the time, Tracey.' He opened the door with a flourish. 'Come on in. It's even better inside.'

She glanced up at him sharply; looked away in some confusion. She wasn't altogether sure yet how she intended the evening to end. Not yet. She stepped inside. Light wood veneer, brightly coloured fabrics, neat kitchen, a real carpet on the floor. A glimpse of bathroom and bedroom discreet behind sliding doors.

'Oh, it's lovely! I wouldn't mind living in one of these all the year round. It's just like a proper home!'

Adrian planted himself on a long low seat, patted the space beside him with a gesture of invitation. Tracey remained standing.

'It wouldn't suit me at all,' he said. 'Not enough space for a start, for all my things. Imagine trying to throw a party in a place this size.'

She sighed. She still thought it would make a lovely little home. Much nicer than the council house her mother had: one of the older ones they kept for problem families and people who got behind with their rent.

'Why, what have you got, then?'

Adrian smiled that lazy smile of his. 'I've got plenty.'

'No, I'm serious. Where do you live? With your mum and dad?'

'Do I look like a bloke who still lives with his mum and dad? Not on your life. I've got a place of my own. A flat.'

'You haven't?'

'Yes, I have. Up in London. Very nice it is, Tracey, very nice indeed.'

'You are lucky, with a car and a place of your own. How do you manage it? It must be ever so expensive.'

Adrian shrugged. 'I can afford it. What's money for, if it's not for spending?' He patted the seat again. It was time for a change of subject. 'I'm surprised you haven't been in one of these places before, Tracey; an attractive girl like you.'

She eyed him thoughtfully. Tracey was becoming a little scared. Playing around with the local boys was one thing. To be alone here with this sophisticated young man was quite another.

'Well I haven't, so there.'

He gave a low whistle. 'Amazing. You must have had a lot of boy-friends, I'm sure.'

She was angry now: 'Are you calling me a liar, Adrian Sheppard?'

'Of course not.' Time to retrench, to hold out a hand, to slip a protective arm around her waist. Pull her down very gently so that she might sit beside him. 'I'm sorry

Tracey. It's just that I feel so jealous of any boy-friend you might have had before I even knew you existed.'

Mollified now, she rubbed her head back against his shoulder.

'I know what you mean,' she whispered. 'I feel just the same way. It's a nice feeling, isn't it?'

Half an hour later Adrian retrieved his left arm from where it was trapped between Tracey's back, and the wall. It had begun to go numb.

'Come.' He took her frozen hand in his. 'Come and see round the place properly: the kitchen, the bathroom; and the bedroom.'

Late evening twilight was falling through high windows into the drawing-room at Goldenacre. Stan lay back in an armchair with his back to the window, Jezebel at his feet, watching Susanne through half-closed eyes: her head haloed in a soft pool of yellow light from an elegant standard lamp. For the last five minutes she had sat with a book open in her lap, and had not turned a single page.

'You're not worried, are you Sue?'

She looked up with a quick smile.

'Yes. I'm becoming the complete neurotic. Adrian first, and now all this. Everything's becoming so complicated. Suppose anyone was to find out?'

'They won't. Not if we're careful. Everything's going to work out just as we planned.'

'I wish I could believe it. I just don't know what to say to Melanie any more, and she will confide in me. It's awful. I'm going to have her on my back all week in the shop.'

'There isn't a lot you can say—just remember that. We're the last people to be able to theorize about Caroline. When they were down at Easter you were up to your eyes getting the salon ready for opening, and we were still being looked on as undesirable aliens then. We never got to know either of them.'

Susanne looked pensive.

'Yes, you're right. I'll have to remind her of that. Chris and Caroline obviously matter a lot to her, but we hardly know them from Adam. That sort of line, you mean?'

Stan nodded. 'Anyhow, Melanie's a lot tougher than anyone seems to give her credit for. Unimaginative, perhaps, but pretty strong, I should think, in a crisis. Russell's the one more likely to go to pieces if you ask me. The poor lad's playing out of his league in trying to emulate that dreadful old father of his. I don't think he's up to taking all the family problems on to his shoulders the way he feels he should. I suppose that's why he and Chris are much closer than most brothers, growing up without a mother in that household.'

Susanne looked round the room as though seeing it for the first time.

'It's a bit creepy to think it all happened here, in this house; in this very room. Those three children growing up together, and all so very different. I used to feel dreadful when any of them came here; like some intruder who'd taken away a terribly important part of their private lives.'

'I think that was true as far as Alex was concerned; probably always will be. But I'm not so sure about Russell. He put Goldenacre on the market remarkably quickly. Almost as though he couldn't wait to have some of those memories obliterated.'

The labrador twitched and raised her head as the phone began to ring out in the hall. Stan went to answer it. Susanne strained to listen. Long periods of silence broken by brief and uninformative responses. When he came back, she raised her eyebrows anxiously.

'That,' he said, 'was Melanie.'

'What's happened?'

'Caroline's car's been found. Abandoned.'

'Where, Stan, where?'

'Up in London. Close to Paddington Station.'

She slumped forward, buried her face in her hands.
'Thank God!'

Jezebel rose and loped over to her; laid a sympathetic
head in her lap. She looked up, half laughing, half
crying.

'Oh, isn't it a relief?' She got up and flew across the
room into Stan's arms. 'You were right all the time! Everything's going to work out after all!'

CHAPTER 5. MONDAY

Susanne's shop did not open till noon on Mondays. All
her life she had dashed off to school or work each Monday
morning, and it had become her favourite indulgence to
start the week with a leisurely family breakfast; then they
would take Jezebel out for a long walk along the sand
dunes before returning to Goldenacre for coffee.

Then, and only then, would she take the footpath
down to the village, and open up the salon.

When she'd first come to Goldenacre Susanne had believed she would never want to work again. Married to
Stan, with a big house and enormous garden, and with all
the money they were ever likely to want, she could see no
reason ever to want an outside job.

She had been wrong.

Years of working and struggling to make something of
her life had left their mark. Both by temperament and
inclination she was one of the world's workers. After a few
weeks the prospect of a lifetime of unstructured time
began to pall. There had to be some contrast. She was
only twenty-five. Different for Stan, already close to
retirement age.

It had been such a relief when she'd been able to talk about it. Where she had been afraid he might be hurt, he had been terrified she might become bored. All her own commercial skill and experience had been in hair-dressing. Stan had sought an interview with the owner of the village salon—she had never liked to ask what sort of an offer he had made—and within weeks she had her own business.

She sat at her desk confronting the weekly paperwork. She hated it. But tomorrow the rep would be calling for her order as he did every three weeks. It lay, neatly typed, in a wire basket. So did the accounts, the bills. At least her turnover was modest enough to ensure that she escaped the nightmare of having to cope with value added tax returns as well. And that was the way she meant to keep it: opening three and a half days a week, with Wednesdays and Saturdays off; a safe and growing trade in regular clients with an upsurge in the season from the tourist traffic. Late night opening on Fridays. A happy balance between her business and her private life.

Melanie, within her limitations, was quite an asset. She was quick and capable, and coped with appointments, cashing up, routine shampooing and sales extremely well. Tracey, on the other hand, would have to go.

Tracey, like Melanie, had come with the business. She might have been satisfactory then, but she was certainly not so any longer. The standard of her work recently had been deplorable, and Susanne was fairly sure she was en-gaged in some light-fingered thieving. She would have to go. Perhaps Angela might like to take over? Earn herself a little pocket money?

At ten to twelve Melanie arrived for work. Already the salon was ready for business: spotless towels to hand, magazines piled neatly on a low table, every one a recent issue; working equipment neatly laid out.

'I was thinking,' said Susanne absently, 'that we really

should get rid of Tracey Harman.'

Melanie hung up her jacket and reached for a green overall. Susanne watched, fascinated, as her thirty-eight-inch bust struggled to get out of her thirty-six-inch blouse.

'Not a moment too soon,' agreed Melanie. 'She'll come to a bad end, that one, if she goes on the way she's doing. I don't like Angela seeing too much of her at all, but it's difficult, when they go to the same school. Right little madam. Boy-crazy. Angela says the boys at school — oh well, never mind.'

Susanne laughed. 'I can imagine what the boys at school say about her, Melanie. You don't need to try to protect me from the harsh realities of life, you know.'

'Well! I mean! And she's only fifteen! After all, it's one thing larking about with boys of her own age, but that Adrian she's going around with is a different proposition altogether. She'll end up in trouble, you mark my words.'

Susanne sat very still. 'I don't think I know him, do I?'

'He's not a local boy. One of the holidaymakers from the caravan site. Quite well-spoken, but a fast worker, I shouldn't be surprised.' She finished doing up the buttons on her overall and fastened the belt. 'Do you want me to ask Angela to tell Tracey you want to see her?'

'Yes,' said Susanne firmly, 'that would be best. Get it over with.'

There was no doubt about it. Tracey Harman would have to go. She brought her thoughts back to the present.

'You've had no more news of Caroline?'

'No. Just the car. They found it in Marylebone. Still had a suitcase in the boot, but no handbag. That may be a good sign — that she's taken it with her somewhere.' She peered into a mirror and combed her hair. 'On the other hand, if she went off on a dirty weekend, why did she leave her case?'

'That's what you think, is it?' asked Susanne with some curiosity.

'Well, of course. It's not the sort of thing you can say to Russell or Alex, but it seems the only answer. I'm very worried about Russell. Seems to think he should dash off to London to be with Christopher. The police seem to be putting him through quite a bad time.'

'It must be very worrying for you all. I tell you someone else who seems badly worried. Geoff Taverner. We saw him in the Green Dragon last night with Toby Wilde.'

Melanie's head was bent over the appointments book.

'He likes her. When Sheila was injured, Caroline was the only person he would talk to about it. Made a sort of bond. He was quite upset that he had to take his holiday early this year, and he'd only see her for a couple of days. That was why we put off our housewarming party until after Chris gets down on Thursday night, Geoff having to go back on Saturday.' She sighed deeply. 'Poor old Geoff.'

Hugh Purcell lowered his spoon into a mug of coffee, allowed the granules of sugar to suck up the liquid until, brown stained, they dissolved into a soggy mass.

'Chris,' he said without looking up. 'Would it be terribly indelicate to ask where the hell you really were on Friday night?'

Chris gave a tired smile. '*Et tu, Brute?*'

'What? Oh, I see. Nice way of telling me to mind my own business.'

Chris moved restlessly on the velvet settee. 'I'm sorry, Hugh.'

'And for God's sake stop fidgeting. You're a keg of nervous energy. Can't be good for you.'

'Father confessor stuff, Hugh? Not at all your style, I'd have thought.'

'Heaven forfend, old son. Forget I mentioned it.'

'I'm sorry. It was good of you to drop in.'

'Impulse thing. Decided to follow you home from school. I'll sod off the moment you say. Didn't like to offer the manly shoulder in the staffroom. A bit public. Everyone walking all round you terrified they might have to say something. Like when that Home Economics lass had her husband die of a heart attack. Conversation died the death the moment she — Oh God! Sorry, Chris. Didn't mean — Look, I'd better go.'

Chris gave a twisted smile. 'No, don't. Stay on a bit. Just so long as you don't start getting paralysed by inhibition. Just try to act natural. It comes easy if you don't think about it.'

There was a small silence, companionable; each man alone with his own thoughts. Then Chris began to talk, as though speaking to himself.

'It's the extraordinary feeling of disorientation, like looking down on the world through the wrong end of a telescope. You can see yourself going through all the right motions like watching yourself acting a part on a distant stage. And you keep expecting to wake up, and find life going on just like it used to. There's nothing finite to come to terms with, like an accident; death even. A sort of suspended animation. I'd almost settle for the relief of knowing, one way or the other.'

Hugh nodded. 'Finding the car hasn't been any help then?'

'It's too early to say, yet. Please God they will find something. Forensics are giving it the once over. Of course they asked me what the mileage had been on the clock. I didn't even know. I did remember it had a service back in the spring; I could even find the bill, but I'd no idea what sort of mileage she'd done since then. Got a nasty feeling they didn't believe me. Only natural they should check things out, of course. It's not hard to realize why. If Caroline . . .' He swallowed. 'If Caroline has been harmed by anyone, it's obvious they must see me as a prime suspect. All those questions, over and over again. Then later on they ask them again, but from a different angle, as though trying to catch you out in some lie. How was it I didn't even know Caroline's closest friends, or where they lived? According to that wretched Helen woman they were on terms of the greatest intimacy, which simply isn't true. She's thoroughly enjoying going round saying she was the last person to see Caroline before she disappeared. Wasn't I alarmed when Caro didn't phone up on Friday? Wasn't it odd that I chose that night to go out for the evening and come home late, and then to take the phone off the hook? You've got to admit it all sounds a bit unlikely, even though it is the truth.'

Hugh kept his eyes firmly on the skin now wrinkling the top of his coffee and resisted all temptation to interrupt the flow of bitterness. Chris had still not finished.

'You've put your finger on the real question, of course. Where I was on Friday night. And I'm telling the truth. I was tired and fed up after a pretty fraught week at school, and I took myself off for a long drive into the country. To Ivinghoe Beacon, in fact. I've always liked the Chilterns. It was a lovely evening, and I stayed there for a long time. But no one believes me. Do you believe me?'

Hugh picked up the challenge. Found there was gravel in his throat, and cleared it away.

'That's a bloody insulting question, if you don't mind my saying so. Of course I believe you. But you're not a complete fool. You know the police have to check out that sort of statement, or they would if — well — wasn't there anyone who saw you, might be able to support your alibi? If it turned out to be necessary, I mean. Did you stop for petrol, or call in anywhere for a drink? There must be someone you can call up as a witness.'

'Oh yes, I had a witness, but not one I'm prepared to call on. Maria Treadwell was with me.'

'Oh my God!'

'I had to, Hugh. If Caroline had been at home, I'd have taken her there, of course, but she wasn't. Maria had told her mother she was babysitting till late, and I did have the sense not to take her back to the flat. The child was almost suicidal. She really needed to talk, and I had to listen, try to calm her down. You'd have done the same.'

'Perhaps.'

Chris stood up, a twisted smile emphasizing the lines of exhaustion around the eyes.

'Hugh, would you mind going home now? I rather think I'm asleep on my feet. And thanks for helping.'

'Me—I've hardly opened my mouth!'

'That's right. Thanks.'

'You're bored silly, aren't you?'

The Green Dragon had been open for business for half an hour, but the evening rush of customers had barely begun. Geoff and Toby were almost alone in the pub garden. Toby planted his pint down on the rustic wooden table.

'Just a bit,' he admitted.

'Not seeing a lot of Alex?'

'It's not just that. I'm not very sure what I'm doing here at all. It's not as though there were any sort of crisis where one could rally round and offer moral support. The whole thing's a bit ridiculous. So the Quinns are a close family, but it strikes me they're all over-reacting like fury.'

'Let's hope you're right.'

'You don't agree?'

Geoff massaged his chin. 'Maybe it's not so easy for me to be objective. I've developed a sort of Jonah complex over the years. See myself as harbinger of disaster and misfortune. Nasty premonitions sloshing away there in my subconscious.'

'But that's absurd!'

'I imagine one of our kind friends has already told you

that I mangled up my wife so badly in a car accident that she's going to be a witless vegetable for the rest of her life?'

Toby ran his index finger up and down the handle of his beer mug.

'Not quite in those terms, but yes, I had heard.' Had Geoff been throwing out an invitation to greater intimacy, or did he just intend to shock? Or were both alternatives a manifestation of the same thing? 'Why do you have to talk about it in that obscene way?'

'Because that's what it was. Obscene. Sheila has become a living obscenity.'

'And it was all your fault?'

'Yes. Alone I did it.'

'Don't you ever talk about it?'

'Just the once. No point after that. Emotional thrashing about is even more obscene. Degrading. Very tedious for one's friends too.'

'Mm, I can see that.' Toby got up. 'Having another?'

'Why not? One way of passing the evening. Nothing happening on the Caroline front. Not down here, anyway.'

As he stood at the bar Toby put in some hard thinking. Geoffrey was right. He was rapidly losing interest in the fate of the missing Caroline. A spot of action might have tempted him to stay on, but action was conspicuous by its absence, and things threatened to get worse. At the same time, he was beginning to become intrigued by the people involved, the personalities, the undercurrents. He still knew very little about them. He could spare another day or so, perhaps. The least he could do for Geoff, poor devil.

He paid for the drinks and sighed. It was a new experience to find he had the beginnings of a social conscience.

The pub garden was filling up fast when he got back.

'Tell me about Caroline Quinn, Geoff.'

His eyes lit up. 'Great girl. Very positive, sort of vibrant.

Not everyone likes her too much, but she's sort of — exciting. Never know what she's going to do next. Impulsive.'

'I find her hard to visualize. The impression I've gained so far is so confused. A mixture of a devoted wife with a track record of being inconsiderate and headstrong, and a sort of *femme fatale* all rolled into one.'

Geoff nodded. 'There's something in that. Perhaps the main thing about Caroline is that she's interesting. She's fun to be with. I'm not talking about sex appeal, though she's got plenty of that; it's something more.'

'The funny thing is,' said Toby, frowning, 'that everybody's eyes light up when they talk about her, just like yours did a minute ago; and yet none of the family seems to show any of that — what would one call it? — affectionate warmth they share with one another. As though they admired her, but weren't terribly fond of her. Even Alex.'

Geoff shot him a quizzical glance. 'Well, I mean, you wouldn't expect her to, now would you?'

'Sorry?'

'Caroline married Chris, didn't she? Being upstaged by another woman doesn't suit Alex too much.'

'Oh!' Toby found himself a little shocked.

'Alex will make a fearsome mother-in-law one day. For the moment she's a fairly formidable sister-in-law. Any woman who married one of her precious brothers was taking up quite a challenge.'

'I'd never thought about it. They all seem to get on so well.'

'Oh yes. Alex is a nice youngster, and if the wives make her brothers happy, that's fine by her. She isn't obviously jealous or anything; just takes it for granted that her links are stronger than theirs will ever be. Families can be rather frightening institutions.'

'How does Melanie cope?'

'With her usual efficiency. Melanie likes everything nicely

ordered. It saves her the trouble of thinking. She has quantified her love very successfully, as she can't compete with the Quinn tradition. Divides her own supply on a seventy-thirty basis between Russell and Angela, who are her very own possessions. Russell gets the lion's share because one day the child will find a husband of her own and the twain will become one flesh. Russell she will have forever.'

Toby's distaste became visible on his face. 'I thought these people were your closest friends?'

'So they are. And they're absolutely fascinating. I love them dearly. Oh come off it, Toby. Your moral principles may do you credit, but analysing our friends is much more fun.'

'What you said about Alex—'

'Alex was virtually brought up by her brothers. When Russell went off to College, it was just her and Chris most of the time. They did everything together. Work it out for yourself.'

'And where does Russell fit in?'

'Russell is almost too good to be true. He's kind and generous and understanding, through and through. Amazingly patient. Was reared on the work ethic and became highly ambitious, though he's never been quite clear what it is he is ambitious for. He gets all his personal fulfilment from his family life. Loves them all, without reservation. Of course, he's monumentally insensitive to their real feelings.'

'But he can't be!'

'Oh yes he is. The love he feels is so simple and straight-forward that he can't envisage any other kind.'

Toby scratched his head. 'You make them all sound very complicated.'

'All interesting people are complicated. That's what makes them interesting. Do you still want to push off to Wales?'

Geoff's face crumpled into that rare smile which was so attractive. Toby laughed.

'Keep talking, and I'll think about it. Give me your in-depth analysis of Christopher.'

'Ah!' Geoff drained his glass. 'Chris is rather an enigma. Much more reserved, more self-contained, than Russell. Quite clever; doesn't miss a lot. A very private sort of man which makes him vulnerable, of course. Not always easy to know what he's thinking. Doesn't show his emotions much. Wears a sort of watchful mask a lot of the time. Very considerate. Nice chap.'

'No hang-ups at all?'

'We've all got hang-ups. Chris doesn't go flaunting his. He's a bit of a Puritan, and can be a bit prickly at times. He's a lucky man to have married Caroline.'

'He is?'

'Oh yes. Just right for each other, those two. The attraction of opposites, or something like that. Whatever it is, it works. Poor devil!'

A young couple crossed the garden, heading for their table. A painfully thin slip of a girl in scarlet jeans, lips and nails to match, dirty bare feet, sharp featured.

'Hello, Geoff! Mind if we join you?'

Geoff looked up and smiled. 'Why, hello Tracey. Nice to see you again. Toby, this is Tracey Harman. Goes to school with Angela.'

Toby nodded agreeably, irritated at the intrusion. He recognized the youth behind her as the one who'd seen him off from Pendrufford Point the day before: twenty-ish, quick easy smile, a certain economy of movement.

'Your friend and I have already met,' he said coldly.

'Oh good. Geoff, this is Adrian. He's staying at the camp site.' She pulled up a chair and sat down. Toby noted with satisfaction that they already carried drinks. He'd be damned if he'd buy one for that young whipper-snapper. Tracey looked up at him from beneath sooted eyelashes. 'So you're Toby? I've been hearing about you. Used to knock around with Alex, did you?' Her eyes were shrewd and knowing.

'Hardly that.'

'Oh, come off it.' She turned her attention to Geoff. 'And how's life been treating you since last year, then? Been taking any more dirty pictures?'

'Hundreds,' he assured her pleasantly.

The girl laughed. 'Geoff here,' she told Adrian, 'has known me nearly all my life.' She patted his knee with easy familiarity. 'Just wanted to say we're sorry to hear about your bit of trouble. You know. The other Mrs Quinn — Caroline. Mum says Mrs Melanie Quinn was talking about it in the shop this afternoon. You're quite sure she didn't come down here?'

'Quite sure, Tracey. Her car has turned up in London.'

She glanced across at Adrian. 'Has it now? We did think, Adrian and me, that she might have been here. Or that you thought she had?'

Geoff's eyes narrowed. 'Why should you think that?'

'Well, Adrian remembered seeing your friend Toby looking through the windows at Pendrufford. We wondered if he might have been looking for her.'

Toby felt it was time to join in the conversation, however briefly.

'Good gracious no.'

'Oh well, if you say so. My mum says she thinks she's probably gone off with another fellow. What do you think, Geoff? After all, you knew her a lot better than most other people, didn't you?'

Geoff shoved his seat back from the table and stood up.

'Nice to have met you again, Tracey. Sorry we can't stay. I trust your friend has a good holiday.'

The two men strode off in the direction of the harbour.

'What a poisonous child your friend Tracey is,' remarked Toby.

'Sad, isn't it, when they turn out that way? Hard to believe that Sheila and I used to build sandcastles with her;
we even taught her to swim. No father, and a slut of a
mother.'

Toby snapped his fingers. 'There was something she
said—I can't quite remember.'

'You don't want to pay any attention to anything
Tracey says.'

'I've got it. Photographs!'

'What?'

'Photographs. You take a lot, Alex said.'

'I play around with it.'

'Have you got one of Caroline? Down here, I mean.'

'Caroline?'

'Yes. So that I can see what she looks like. It would
make her more—more tangible, somehow.'

'I've got a batch of shots I took last year. Didn't get
them developed in time to show them off then. I'll look
them out when we get back.' He picked up a flat pebble
and sent it spinning across the water. 'I take it you mean
to stay on for a day or two?'

In a lay-by a mile or so out of the village on the Port
Laverock road a bright red telephone box stood back
from the road against a thicket of greenery. Inside it
Adrian and Tracey faced each other, squashed together
in some discomfort.

'Lay off, Adrian, will you?'

'I thought you liked it?'

'Not here. Not now. Someone might see us.' She looked
up, childlike, suddenly anxious. 'You're quite sure we
ought to?'

'Why not? They'll never know it was us.'

'Are you sure? I mean, I don't want any trouble.'

'Not a chance. My voice won't mean a thing to him.
Anyway, we'll be doing him a favour. Ought to liven

things up quite a bit.'

'Oh, I don't know.'

'For the love of Mike! You drag me all the way up here—'

'Yes, all right, Adrian. I like him, d'you see? He's always been very nice to me.'

'Well, there you are then. You'll be helping him.'

'You're quite sure?'

'Sure I'm sure. Now what's the number?'

'You won't forget to press the knob so that he won't know we're using a phone box?'

'I'm not a complete idiot, Tracey.'

'No.' Still uncertain. 'Suppose he's not in?'

'Then we lose our money. My money, as it happens.'

'Suppose they come asking questions.'

'They're bound to. We just say we don't know any-thing. Remember that, Tracey. We don't know a thing.'

'Right.' She glanced nervously over her shoulder. 'Right, you'd better get on with it then. Get it over with.'

Adrian made a pile of coins on top of the directory box, consulted the scrap of paper Tracey had been clutching in her hand and began to dial 01 for London.

CHAPTER 6. TUESDAY

A finger of light crept through a crack in the bedroom curtains and danced along the bedspread, quivering, exploring. Geoff watched it with hot, tired eyes. Three o'clock in the morning and he was still awake, tossing and turning, thoughts grinding incessantly round in his mind.

In a sudden movement he threw back the bedclothes and put his bare feet on the floor. Rubbed his eyes, ran the fingers of both hands through thick dark hair. Pulled back the curtains from the small sash window and stared out at the sea. The tide was so far out that there was no sound of waves dredging over the gravelled shore. Only a flat expanse of wet and shining sand.

The floorboards always creaked abominably, never more so than in the middle of the night, and he had a guest asleep next door. With infinite care he picked up his clothes and tiptoed out, down the outside of the stair treads to the room downstairs. Dressed, thrust his feet into salt-stained beach shoes and slipped silently out by the front door.

His shadow fell behind him, sharp and clear, as he crossed the tarmac road to the shore, over hummocks of grass and dry, slippery sand; and ran over high banked shells and seaweed of the highest strandline down to the sea.

Here were wormcasts, which he squashed beneath his feet, and harder sand, rippled, puddled. He slipped off his shoes and allowed his toes to wriggle down among the wet cold gritty grains, digging out small and squelchy holes that filled with water. Tiny flat waves broke over his feet; soon they would gather strength to grow in force and sweep in once more to cover the vastness of the bay.

Geoff rolled his trouser legs above the knee and paddled out. Looked back at the village nestled round its harbour. Looked ahead to Pendrufford Point, black and rocky. No one, not even a lone fisherman, was in sight. He set off towards it.

It was ridiculous, childish, he told himself, for a grown man to behave like this: to feel the need to make a sort of pilgrimage. To exorcize for all time the shades of the past. Sheer mawkish sentimentality. He kept going.

There was no one, now, who knew that they had planned to buy Pendrufford. It had been Sheila's idea, when they had honeymooned there eight summers ago. She'd been an art teacher in those days. Wouldn't it be marvellous, she'd said idly, if we could turn a place like this into a craft centre? Make a pottery out of that derelict out-building? Geoff could go on working at some bank nearby while she would run the place. Perhaps it would be so successful that he'd be able to pack up his job altogether?

It had all been a daydream then, light-hearted and casual. Later on they talked it over seriously. Why not? Perhaps they might not get Pendrufford, but somewhere like it. They started to economize, to save, to study the logistics of running a small business. Each year they came down on holiday and planned how they would adapt the house to suit their purpose. The owner lived somewhere up country, and might be prepared to sell if they made him a decent offer. Next year. No children yet. A family could wait until they could bring them up the way they wanted.

It took them almost four years before they felt able to realize the dream; and only seconds to destroy it, in a screech of tearing metal, scorching tyres and awful silence.

Geoff had never been inside Pendrufford since. Chris and Caroline, grown more prosperous, had rented it for the whole summer instead of staying at Goldenacre. And now they had bought it, outright, with a legacy from his father. Geoff had only found out last week, and had been consumed with savage jealousy ever since.

Caroline had understood. She was the only person who had ever understood a little of how he felt. But she had still agreed to buy Pendrufford.

The long, deliberate walk through the water was strangely healing. At the headland he waded out on to the rocks and pulled on his shoes. A jutting spur, rough with barnacles, tore at his leg, and blood began to trickle down from the graze. He dabbed at it with his sleeve, scrambled up on to the shelf of short cropped grass.

Odd how one could look at a house, and still not see it. Only be aware, with painful intensity, of the essence of a

love-affair from long ago. Pendrufford, as a shrine, had
served its purpose.

One final indulgence, a concession to nostalgia.

Past the front of the small stone house, round to the out-
building with one door still hanging loose from its hinges.
The front door key would be there, under the usual flower-
pot. He would go back, just this once, before everything
was changed.

He pulled back the trailing door.

Inside was a grey Volkswagen.

Geoffrey Taverner stood very still.

Tracey drank her tea and snuggled back under the bedclothes. No school for her today. Her mother had fallen
for that story about the violent stomach pains which had
kept her awake half the night, and had now gone off to
her cleaning job up Mafia Mews. Plenty of work going
there now the schools were breaking up. All those people
with their flash cars and bossy voices. Mum would be all
right, so long as the social security people didn't get to
hear of it. You could never tell, in a place like this.
Always someone ready to put the boot in.

During the long dark evenings of the previous winter,
Tracey had discovered the enchanted world of romantic
fiction, and grown addicted to that alien lifestyle. In the
intimacy of her own room she had embarked on the cre-
ation of a fantasy existence where men were strong and
tender, and lived a jet set life of money and leisure and
constant travel. When the careers staff at school hounded
her about what she really planned to do, she would shrug
them off with vague talk about becoming a beautician.
That seemed to keep them happy. Easy to convince them
that Mrs Hyson was prepared to put in a good word for
her among some of her London contacts. When the time
came.

For the moment, however, there was Adrian. Quite the

most fascinating man she'd ever been out with. Quite a posh voice, goodlooking, plenty of money; and a flat of his own in London. Believed in being his own boss too. You can get anything you want in life, darling, he'd told her, if you're prepared to pay the price.

Tracey had savoured the word darling, and had paid.

There was something mysterious about Adrian too. With all that money, what was he doing in a caravan when he could afford any of the best hotels? Strange, too, that he was on his own, without any mates, or a girlfriend of his own. He'd been very cagey about his private life, and Tracey hadn't pressed him. She knew that boys got quite uptight if you pretended you weren't interested, and ended up telling you all you wanted to know just to make an impression.

But Adrian wasn't like that. He'd just grin at her and say nothing. He had a lovely smile. Intriguing. She was going to see him again at lunch-time.

Meanwhile, she'd better see Mrs Hyson. Even that didn't worry her too much any more. She could deal with Mrs Hyson. Thanks to Adrian.

The salon was busy when she arrived. Two women already under the dryer, two waiting and another being shampooed. Susanne was working single-handed. Tracey hesitated in the doorway.

'I hear you wanted to see me, Mrs Hyson?'

Susanne's eyebrows went up. 'Not at school today then, Tracey?'

'I had a terrible headache—stomach ache, I mean. It's a bit better now.'

'That's good—whichever it was.'

Tracey glanced round. 'Where's Mrs Quinn?'

'She is not in this morning. Now will you go through to the office, Tracey? I'll be with you as soon as I'm free.'

'What's the matter with Mrs Quinn? Has there been some news about Caroline?'

The two waiting women exchanged glances and bent their heads over magazines. The lady being shampooed cleared her left ear of suds.

'I have no idea.' Susanne's voice was crisp. 'Now please do as I ask, and wait next door.'

Tracey cast her a baleful glance, strode across the shop and flung herself into the office chair. Voices rose and fell as the minutes ticked by. When Susanne came in her manner was distant and severe.

'Right, Tracey. You're not going to like this very much, but it won't take long. I'm afraid I can't employ you any longer on Saturdays. I'm sorry, but your standard of work simply isn't good enough.'

Tracey's eyes disappeared into resentful slits. There was not a sound from the salon, and she could visualize the four incumbents sitting with heads craned forward, trying to eavesdrop on the exchange. She raised her voice.

'Oh come now, Mrs Hyson,' she said in honeyed tones. 'Don't you think you might be making a mistake? Or I might tell you something that you wouldn't like too much either.'

Susanne stiffened. Good. That would shake her.

The shop door pinged as more people came into the shop. Fantastic! Let them all hear.

'You see, Mrs Hyson—' she gave her employer a sly smile— 'I've got a new boy-friend. He's called Adrian.'

'Look, Tracey—'

'There are quite a lot of things we might talk about, Mrs Hyson. I don't suppose we were the only ones who thought Malcolm was late on his round on Friday, if you see what I mean.'

Although she had spoken very clearly, the effect of this was lost in the appearance in the doorway, not of the next client, but of Melanie, smiling broadly.

'Look who's here!' she cried. Behind her came Alex and Christopher Quinn.

Susanne held out her hands.

'Chris! How very nice to see you. When did you get here?'

'In the early hours of this morning sometime.' He lowered his voice and glanced back at the salon. 'We'll tell you all about it later, when we don't have an audience.' He smiled at Tracey. 'Nice to see you again too. How are you?'

'I'm fine, thanks. You're quite right, you know. It's surprising what people can overhear in a place like this. Best to play it safe.' She looked up at him anxiously. 'You haven't found your wife yet, have you?'

'I'm afraid not. But it was kind of you to ask.'

Susanne cut in sharply. 'Tracey's not at all well today, Chris. She's been quite badly ill, and I think she should go straight home and take care of herself. Off you go, Tracey. We all hope you'll feel much better soon.'

The girl glared at her, regained her composure and stood up.

'All right then, Mrs Hyson. I'll be in as usual on Saturday.' A statement, not a question.

For a moment Susanne hesitated.

'We'll talk about it later, Tracey.'

Tracey stopped in the doorway.

'Oh I don't think there's any need, do you?'

Toby kicked open the front door, hot pasties wrapped in newspaper held beneath his chin on top of half a dozen beer cans.

'Lunch-time! Lovely hot pasties!'

Geoff eyed him sourly from a position of comfort on the couch.

'You're going to drop that lot. I thought we were going to have something decent, like fish and chips?'

'Get up, you idle lump, and get some plates, will you?' He stacked the cans of beer on the Formica table. 'Sorry about the fish, but by the time I got there, they were closed. I ran into Alex. Christopher Quinn's arrived.'

'Has he now?' Geoff reached two plates down from the rack above the cooker. He had been preparing all morning for this moment, and turned round eagerly, 'Is Caroline with him?'

'Afraid not. But he got a phone call last night—an anonymous one—saying her car was seen down here heading along the Pendrufford track last Friday evening. A small red Fiat.'

Geoff pursed his lips.

'That's right. She had one of those last year—present from her parents. But she can't have been down here—can she?'

'I've no idea.' Toby shovelled the pasties out of their wrappings on to the plates and sat down. 'Probably one of those malicious calls made by some crank. That's all he needs.'

'A man or a woman?'

'A man, apparently. Come on, eat that damn thing before it's cold.' He inspected his own with some suspicion 'I don't think I want to know what they put inside them.'

Geoff zipped the top from a beer can and drank deeply.

'So that's what brought him down, was it? An anonymous phone call. Has he managed to trace it, or found anything to suggest that Caroline really was here?'

'Not so far as I know. Seems he rang Russell right away and then drove straight to Pendrufford. Alex seems to think it's all a wild goose chase, what with the car being found in London. Unless—' he masticated a large mouthful with some care— 'someone drove it back. She could even have done it herself, I suppose. But goodness knows why she should come all that way, and then turn round and go back. She could have come down to see someone, perhaps?'

Geoff's face crumpled into that warm smile Toby was becoming used to. 'I was wondering how long you would be able to resist it.'

'Resist what?'

'Playing detectives.'

'Don't be so ridiculous.'

'Have it your own way. Everybody else has got a theory. Melanie's putting her faith in some unknown man of irresistible charm who's swept her off to his love-nest somewhere.'

'How d'you know that?'

'That's what she told Susanne.'

'My God! It's a conspiracy. Do you all go round reporting on your friends' private conversations like this?'

Geoff grunted. 'What a sensitive soul you are, Toby. Of course we talk about them. It's not just malicious gossip, not with Susanne, at any rate. She and Stan and I are involved up to a point, but we're not family. So perhaps we can see things a bit more clearly than they can. It also helps us to help them, if we know what they think, privately. It should be easier for you than anyone. After all, you're a complete outsider.'

'Thanks a lot. I think you're becoming quite obsessional, all of you. Creating a great melodrama out of nothing at all. Must come from living in a place like this where nothing ever happens. I just think it's a bit off to go discussing them with Susanne and Stan—you hardly know them.'

Geoff licked his fingers. 'You've got a point there. I'd never set eyes on them till this summer; but Alex and I have spent a lot of time with them, playing tennis and sailing. Nice couple. I stand rebuked. You won't want to hear what Russell thinks?'

'Well—' Toby struggled with his finer feelings, and lost.

'Russell's not saying much at all. Doesn't want to upset

Melanie, but Stan thinks he's prepared for the worst. Like she was surprised by some roving maniac, probably on the way to Bournemouth, who did something rather nasty and then drove the car back to London and abandoned it. I'm terribly afraid he might be right. It would fit in with all the evidence.'

'Evidence? What evidence? There isn't any.'

'Exactly. That's why the police are so interested in Chris, I should think. As Angela said, husbands by tradition become first suspects. Anyone who knows Chris would find his story hard to swallow. All that garbage about imagining she was staying with a friend, and going off till all hours to Ivinghoe Beacon. I bet the police are taking a good look through any undergrowth out that way.'

Toby looked at him with some repugnance. 'You're not accusing Chris of murdering his wife?'

'Of course I'm not, you young fool. I'm just trying to look at the facts with some objectivity. That should appeal to your nice tidy legal mind. If that anonymous phone call was true, and Caroline was down here on Friday, that lets Chris out completely. He couldn't have driven here and back between leaving school around six and being wakened by the police at eight next morning.' He frowned. 'Or could he? Thirteen, fourteen hours? A round trip of over five hundred miles? And disposed of—of the evidence and all that as well?'

The two men looked at each other unhappily.

'It would be possible,' conceded Toby at length, 'but he'd have to be going some, and those small Fiats don't have a lot of power, do they?'

Geoff took their plates over to the sink.

'Perhaps you're right,' her said abruptly. 'Perhaps we shouldn't go digging around too much. Never know what you might find.'

He fell silent as he rinsed the plates, put them on the rack to dry. Toby would have given a lot to know what he was thinking, and let his gaze wander round the room, typical of a holiday cottage rented out to summer visitors. Basic functional furnishings in one big room taking up the whole of the ground floor: sitting area, table with four chairs, kitchen unit. Narrow boxed stairs leading up to two bedrooms, the third converted into small bathroom with shower. Stark and simple, with none of the charm of Shrimp Cottage next door. No pictures or ornaments or flowers. Just their jackets hanging from hooks on the wall, alongside binoculars, a camera. A camera.

'You were going to let me see those photographs of Caroline.'

'What?'

'The photographs you took of Caroline last year.'

Geoff pitched his empty beer can into a plastic binette.

'Oh yes. Sure. I've got them upstairs somewhere.'

He vanished up the narrow staircase. Toby could hear him moving around, opening and closing drawers. He came back holding two prints, and handed the first over with some pride: a family group, relaxed though obviously posed. Russell sitting on a beach with one arm round Melanie, the other round Angela. Behind them stood Alex with the couple he had heard so much about.

He studied it with macabre interest. Christopher Quinn was unmistakably Russell's brother, but of leaner build, a tall, spare man whose smile towards the camera was less spontaneous, more tentative. His wife was laughing up at him, her arm round his waist, head thrown back.

Everything he had heard about Caroline was true. An immediately attractive girl with a lovely face and splendid figure, alive with personality.

'She's lovely,' he said quietly. 'Quite beautiful.'

'Yes. This is another one I'm rather fond of.'

The second print was a head and shoulders shot of Caroline alone: caught unawares in a moment of abstraction, thoughtful, half smiling, hair blown back in disorder from her face; a fine, intelligent face.

'That's Caroline, not playing to the gallery for once.' The fond expression on Geoff's face robbed the words of any sting. 'I snapped her while she was watching Chris trying to lower the sail of their dinghy in a howling gale. It's exactly like her.'

Toby stared at it, fascinated, for a long time. When he handed it back, his manner had changed entirely.

'I wish I hadn't seen them. I should never have asked.'

Geoff smiled sadly. 'So we're all absolved from over-reacting, from becoming obsessional?'

'Yes, I'm sorry. Until now I've been able to think of her as a sort of abstraction, a disembodied presence. I could feel decently sympathetic, but it didn't really register.' He rose and walked about restlessly; took off his glasses, polished them on his shirt and put them back on. 'When I saw Alex she asked me to tell you we were invited up to Goldenacre this evening. Nothing special. A sort of welcome home for Chris, if that's not a ghastly way of putting it. Susanne thought Melanie had enough to cope with already, and it might take the pressure off her for one night.'

'Considerate pair, the Hysons.'

'Yes. I shan't be going, of course. I've gone right off the idea of taking up voyeurism as a holiday entertainment.'

Geoff gave a sardonic snort. 'You know what you are, Toby? You're a pompous young ass. And as long as you're my guest you'll damn well accept any invitations from my friends which happen to include you. Or you can get on your bike and get to hell out of here just as soon as you like.'

As the first set of the evening approached its end, Stan smiled down at his wife and squeezed her hand.

'Your machinations seem to be working,' he said softly.

Susanne glanced quickly across to where Chris and

Alex lay sprawled on the grass, watching the tennis.

'They do, don't they? Violent exercise is far more useful than hushed voices and manly grips on the shoulder for anyone under stress. And doesn't Melanie play well? She and Russell have been running rings round Geoff and Toby.' She sighed. 'Isn't there anything that woman can't do if she sets her mind to it?'

Stan laughed. 'She's a tactician. Plans her game and conserves her energy. But it's Chris who needs your therapy more than anyone. Just look at him — like a coiled spring. He's had a basinful of people down here becoming screwed up with a sympathy they don't know how to express.'

'Mm. Let's hope it works.'

Susanne's eyes were troubled. There had already been a spell of agonizing tension when the various couples had arrived: Russell first, with Melanie, anxious that they might be too early; then Geoff with Toby, looking very much as though he were there under protest. It was when Alex arrived with Chris that the atmosphere became infused with a false conviviality, as though the curtain had risen on stage characters who had forgotten their lines and were improvising until rescued by some unseen prompter: brittle as finest glass.

Russell was slapping Geoff on the back as they came, panting, off the Goldenacre court.

'Great game, you two!' He caught his breath and was seized by a spasm of coughing. Melanie frowned. 'Out of condition, that's my trouble.' He laughed ruefully as he recovered. 'We ought to have had a bet on the result, you know. Suppose we lay bets on the next game, everyone?'

Chris scrambled to his feet.

'No thanks. I never did have your unerring instinct for gambling. Come along, Alex. Let's see if we can be ill-mannered enough to make mincemeat of our hosts.'

Melanie sat down heavily in a deckchair next to Toby.

'Susanne, I forgot to ask. Did you ever get round to sacking young Tracey Harman?'

Susanne bent to pick up her racquet.

'Yes, I did,' she said shortly.

'Good thing too. Right little madam she's turned into. Heading for trouble, that one, if I'm any judge. Up to no good at all with that boy from the caravan site—an extremely unpleasant young man, in my opinion.'

Russell, in the act of lighting a cigarette, caught the smoke at the back of his throat and began another coughing fit. Melanie snatched the cigarette from him and ground it out in an ashtray; poured him a glass of orangeade and held it out. Susanne exchanged a quick glance with Stan, who put an arm round her shoulder as they walked over to join Chris and Alex on court.

Russell drank deeply, recovered his breath, and turned to Toby.

'Look, I've been doing a lot of thinking about Caroline. Would you mind giving me a couple of straight answers while Chris is safely out of earshot?'

'If I can. I'm not an authority on missing persons.'

'Fair enough. But is it likely that the longer she stays missing, the greater the chance that there may have been some sort of foul play?'

Toby considered this. 'Probably yes. Failing any good reason why she might have wanted to disappear of her own accord.'

'And the chance of identifying the guilty party?'

'That would get less too. Unless there were witnesses. Very difficult to solve, cases like that, where there isn't any evidence or suggestion of motive. Even when the police have a strong suspect, if there's no evidence or statement of admission, there's not a lot they can do.'

'But that's outrageous!' said Melanie.

'It's the law, I'm afraid. In this country a man is innocent until proved guilty; that means the jury must be convinced beyond any reasonable doubt—you know how it goes. If there is no evidence and no confession, there's no case. It's as simple as that.'

Russell shook his head and looked unhappy.

'Thanks, Toby. It's best that we should be prepared, don't you think? Just in case?'

'You don't have to walk all the way back with me, you know.'

Alex looked up at her brother. 'Would you rather I didn't?'

'Good Lord no!'

'Because if you'd rather be alone, you've only got to say.'

'I know that, Alex. But it's been a very pleasant evening, and it would make a nice ending.'

'Oh good. What did you think of Susanne?'

'Very attractive; thoughtful, too. You could see she found the whole thing a bit of a strain, but worked very hard not to let it show.'

'Why should she be under a strain?'

Chris laughed. 'Dearest Alex. Just having me around is a terrible strain on anyone, I'm beginning to discover. Even Melanie. Especially Melanie. I'm mucking up her nicely ordered little world quite horribly. It's taken me all day to persuade her that the last thing I want is to move into her spare bedroom. Bless her heart. She's a good-hearted soul.'

Alex reached out and took his hand.

'Yes, I heard you. Russell managed to put her off the idea without hurting her feelings.'

'She's quite amazing. Never changes. Do you know she even went over to Pendrufford one day last week and springcleaned the whole place out ready for our arrival. It was a good thing Caroline didn't know. She'd really have blown her top.'

Alex giggled; squeezed his hand.

They stopped by the harbour; leant over the wall to watch the boats.

'I like being back,' said Chris. 'There's a sort of security in familiar places and people. In London I felt sort of threatened. No one knew what to say to me. Which way shall we go — lane or shore?'

'The tide's just about on the turn although it's still quite high. What the hell — let's go by the shore.'

They climbed down the steps by the harbour wall on to the pebbled part of the beach. The sky was taking on that cool translucent glow which comes with early twilight. There were few people about; just a couple of men walking dogs. Children were in bed, adults in the Green Dragon. A few scavenging gulls paced the strandline.

At high tide the walk around the bay was nearly a mile long. Both were bright-eyed and breathless when they reached the point. Chris scrambled up the gully first, held out his hand to pull his sister after him.

'Coming in for a coffee?'

'No, thanks. I'm going to do my maternal bit and let you go straight to bed. I'll go back by the lane.'

'Good night, Alex. Thanks for coming.'

'Good night, Chris. Sleep well.'

She walked away, a few steps along the headland. Stopped and stared. Let out a small gasp. Clapped the palms of her hands to the sides of her face.

'Chris?'

'Yes?'

'Come here.'

He ran to her side, eyes following her pointing finger down to where deep water lapped quietly along the sides of the gully.

Where a body floated gently, face downward, hair trailing like fronds of dark seaweed, bumping against the rock.

He slithered down the scree on to the rock, reached out and drew it clear of the water.

'It's Caroline?' whispered Alex.

He shook his head.

'No. It's not Caroline. It's Tracey. Tracey Harman.'

CHAPTER 7. WEDNESDAY

By breakfast-time next morning the news had spread through the village with the rapidity of a forest fire. So had the police, travelling in couples from door to door, enquiring, noting, recording. Locals who had not spoken for years were seen talking in pairs, in groups, with pursed lips, nodding heads; vying with one another in their claims to have seen young Tracey — spoken with her even — only yesterday.

Holidaymakers found themselves caught up in the sensation; looked in awed fascination across the bay to Pendrufford Point, now sealed off against the public; wondered how soon it might be seemly to take a boat out and take a closer look at the scene of the crime; drew their children closer to them. A maniac, they were saying. No young girl was safe these days.

Curtains stayed drawn at the windows in the clutch of council houses close to Mrs Harman's home, poor thing, as a mark of respect. Neighbours pondered the thought of knocking at her door in case there was anything they could do, anything they might hear which was not already common knowledge. By eight o'clock the finger of suspicion was pointing firmly towards the caravan site: to number twenty-three, rented by a young man from London. Adrian Sheppard had not been home all night.

In the blue and white kitchen at The Shrubberies, Melanie put a rack of toast in front of her daughter. Her homely face ached with concern.

'Angela, you really must try to eat something. Just to please me?'

'No, thanks, Mummy. I'm feeling a bit sick.'

'Of course you do. We all do. Are you quite sure you want to go to school? After all, it is the last day. You won't be missing much.'

'I'll be all right, honestly.' She smiled bleakly. 'We get our end of term reports today. I wonder what they'll do with Tracey's? It wouldn't be much fun for her mother to find out what she was really like.'

'I'm sure the headmaster will think of that, dear.'

'I feel awful about all those things I said about her yesterday on the school bus. She took the day off, you know, so that she could have lunch with Adrian. Said she had some tummy bug, but everyone knew what she was really up to.'

'If you ask me,' said her mother darkly, 'the police will be taking a close interest in that young man.'

Russell came into the room, dressed for work; dropped a kiss on his daughter's forehead and slid into his seat.

'Daddy, you look dreadful! Have you been up all night? You should have woken me.'

He smiled at her.

'Not all night, love. But I spent a fair bit of it with Chris and Alex. They both went back to Shrimp Cottage after making statements to the police. It was a terrible experience for them, finding Tracey like that.'

Angela stared at him, open-mouthed.

'You mean it was Chris who found the body? Mummy never told me that. That's quite serious, isn't it?'

'Not very nice at all.' Russell reached for the toast as Melanie poured coffee into his cup.

'I mean—police are always very interested in people who report finding dead bodies. And with the Caroline business as well—'

'Angela!' Melanie's tone was sharp. 'That's quite enough of that. You must be very careful what you go around saying to people. You must remember that real life is not at all like those thrillers you're always reading.'

'It's true though, Mummy.' Her voice was subdued. 'I wish I'd liked Tracey a bit more. I'd be sorrier, of course, but it would be more comfortable.'

'Let's not pretend, Angela,' said her father. 'Tracey was not always—well—' He floundered and began again. 'You must not reproach yourself. Why, even your mother was speaking rather unkindly about her last night at Susanne's.'

'That's true, dear. When I think I told Susanne it was high time we gave her the sack, I feel pretty awful too. Poor child.'

Angela reached out absently for a slice of toast.

'I suppose it wouldn't be much fun if we all went around being terribly nice to everybody just in case they dropped dead on us.'

Her parents exchanged worried glances above her head.

'Now you mustn't allow yourself to become morbid, dear,' said Melanie. 'Life still has to go on, you know.'

'Not for Tracey it doesn't. I suppose she actually was killed, was she? She didn't just drown—sort of naturally?'

Russell's eyes met hers; he put out a hand to stroke her cheek with tenderness.

'I'm afraid not, Angela. It seems she was strangled before being found in the water.'

'Just think,' said Geoff, 'you might have been a keen young minion of the law like that. I thought you handled it all very well.'

Toby reacted with irritation. 'What's that supposed to mean?'

'Nothing, Toby, nothing at all. All those tricky questions about Christopher and Alex. You put me in mind of the three wise monkeys, all of whose friends must have been quite above reproach as well. Like Cæsar's wife.'

'Well, so they are, as far as I know. We can't expect to be told what evidence the police may have discovered.'

'Yes—shame, isn't it? We don't really know what to think. Very confusing.'

'Surely there was no need for you to describe Tracey as the local *fille de joie*? That younger copper had no idea what you were talking about.'

'*De mortuis nil nisi bonum* and all that? You're not the only one with a bit of education around here. Anyway, I wasn't speaking ill of anyone; only telling the truth. They'd find that out sooner or later, believe me. Melanie was always saying that poor wretched child would come to a bad end.'

Toby stared hard at him.

'You're a callous brute, aren't you?'

Geoff stared straight back, jaw pushed forward.

'You're so unspeakably naïve, Toby, so totally wet behind the ears. When you've grown up a bit you'll find that there are two fairly classic reactions to dreadful news. Most people are shocked and stunned, and may be able to find relief in tears; but some of us resort to sick humour and bad jokes. All very aggressive and in terribly bad taste. Very embarrassing for other people to cope with.'

'I'm sorry.'

'No need. Just remember you might meet that sort of reaction again one day.' He moved restlessly round the room. 'I've known Tracey since before she joined the Brownies.' He smiled. 'They drummed her out after three weeks. D'you still want to push off to Wales?'

'Well—'

'Now that we've got a real live murder—Oh God!—a real murder on our doorstep with your girl-friend virtually tripping over the body? Appeals to you, does it? Make some coffee, will you?'

Toby moved obediently to the sink.

'Do you want me to stay?'

'You can please yourself. Only till Saturday, of course. I've got to vacate the place that morning.'

'Thanks.' Toby unscrewed the top from a jar of instant coffee. 'Has it occurred to you that somebody might be trying to throw suspicion on Christopher Quinn? The Pendrufford connection? My God, it sounds like a cheap thriller. But if that anonymous phone call was true, and Caroline was over there on Friday . . .'

'That singularly unpleasant thought had crossed my mind, as it happens. Except that we only have Chris's word for it that there was a phone call at all, remember? And if there were, it could have been a hoax. Of course it's wicked to start jumping to conclusions, but I should think the lad Adrian will be in for some close attention. And Tracey could always have died at the hands of some sex maniac down here on holiday. That sort of thing does happen.'

Toby shook his head. 'Too many maniacs. One for Caroline, according to Russell's line of questioning last night. Another one for Tracey?'

'Dodgy, that. We keep coming back to that phone call. If it were true, then things are going to get very unpleasant. There will be a lot of alibi checking going on.'

Toby brought over two mugs of steaming coffee; joined Geoff at the other end of the couch.

'Alibis can always be faked. Take us—at Susanne's last night. Eight people who can all vouch for one another during the time we were there. But outside of those hours, from around eight till about ten, just look at the neat way we can be paired off: Stan and Susanne, Russell and Melanie, Alex and Chris, you and me. Each pair—except for us—apparently devoted to each other. So if any of

them were working in cahoots, their alibis wouldn't be
worth a light.'

'And if they weren't covering up for each other—if any
one of us working alone were involved in some sort of
skulduggery?'

Toby scratched his head. 'It would depend. Alibis provided by one's nearest and dearest tend to be a bit suspect
at the best of times. Added to that, people who live together
tend to take a lot for granted. They assume their partners
are where they claimed to be as they have no reason to
doubt it. I should think that's even more true in a place
like this in high summer than it is in the towns and sub-
urbs. People wander about the countryside, or take a
walk along the beach, or pop in on friends, in a way that
doesn't happen in cities. No one gives it a second
thought.'

There was a gleam of excitement in Geoffrey's eyes.

'My word, you are coming on! Keep talking, Toby. You
may not believe this, but I have a strong urge to see the
man who killed young Tracey clapped behind bars for the
rest of his life.'

There was nothing Adrian Sheppard found more enjoyable than a night out with some kindred spirits engaged
in the downing of quantities of real ale; an indulgence for
which a price had to be paid, as with everything worth
having in this life. It manifested itself in a certain fragility
around the temples and a reluctance to contemplate the
condition of his alimentary canal. Sleeping the night
away in the back of his car had not helped very much
either, but the chance of being breathalysed was not one
he'd been prepared to take.

He turned off right from the Treskellan road into the
lane which led back to the caravan site: a very pleasant
place to spend a holiday, small and exclusive with self-
catering homes sited each in its own small garden, all

beautifully maintained. None of those regimented rows of caravans banked three and four deep which littered so many of the coastal areas of Cornwall and Devon. It had been an ideal choice, pretty and secluded, with no hotel staff or landlady to breathe down his neck, take an interest in his movements.

Three children playing outside the next door caravan looked up from their game as he drew up and parked. He smiled and waved, but not before they had turned and gone scampering back through their own front door.

A prickle of unease ran down his spine. They were a friendly bunch of kids; a bit of a nuisance at times. What had got into them, all of a sudden?

He left the door standing open and went through the van opening all the windows, tipped his supplies from a carrier bag on to the kitchen draining-board: bread, milk, eggs; sausages and a tin of beans for when he felt better, and an apple pie. He began to unbutton his crumpled shirt.

'Mr Sheppard?'

The prickle of apprehension jabbed more sharply.

'Mr Adrian Sheppard?'

A man looking up at him through the caravan door, head tilted to one side, with the expression of a visiting clergyman. Behind him stood his sidekick.

The law had come to call. Pleasant and courteous, unlike the heavy mob, but the law just the same.

'Yes. What can I do for you?'

Cards were displayed. Detective-Inspector Bracken, Detective-Sergeant Golspie. From Port Laverock. An inspector, no less. Adrian lifted his eyebrows in bewilderment.

'Just making a few routine enquiries, Mr Sheppard. Mind if we come in?'

'No, of course not. Take a seat. What's up?'

For the first time he regretted his over-indulgence in

real ale. Its effect, twelve hours later, was no help at all in trying to make a snap assessment of the situation. They might be country coppers, but it would be unwise to underestimate them. Inspector Bracken, forty-ish, sharp-eyed, small moustache, the beginnings of a paunch; and with the bedside manner of the doctor who made his living from private patients. His sergeant, younger, scrawny, earnest, watchful. Neither of them had accepted his invitation to sit down. No social call, this. Right. Leave them to do the talking.

'You've been away then, Mr Sheppard?'

He turned bewildered eyes on them. 'Yes. Why—have I missed something?'

'Would you mind telling us where you were last night?'

'No, of course not. I was in Torquay.'

'And around what time did you leave Treskellan?'

Adrian gestured vaguely: 'Oooh, must have been some time between two and three yesterday afternoon.'

He was beginning to feel happier; smiled at the silent sergeant who didn't seem quite sure whether he ought to smile back. A bad sign.

'Any particular reason for going to Torquay?'

Adrian never went in for direct lies where he could avoid them. 'Well—' he shrugged— 'no particular reason except that's where all the action is in the West Country, isn't it? Bright lights, girls, all that. You've got to admit there isn't much in the way of nightlife here in Treskellan, is there?'

'Newquay is a lot nearer,' suggested the Inspector.

'Look, mate, I'm on holiday! I've already done the Newquay scene. What's this all about, anyhow?'

'All in good time, sir. So you spent the night in Torquay?'

'Well, somewhere near there.' He was being invited to enlarge on his story. He opened the fridge door and put the milk and sausages inside. Gave a small shamefaced laugh. 'Met up with some lads on the front, picked up some girls and went on a bit of a pub crawl.'

Inspector Bracken gave an understanding nod; said nothing.

'Well, that's all, really. Ended up getting fairly well stoned, and spent the night in the car in a lay-by just outside the town. Didn't feel too bright when I woke up, drove back to Plymouth. Didn't think too much of the place, so after a look round the Hoe, I came on back here.'

Question marks of doubt were writ large in invisible ink on two impassive foreheads. Was he talking too much? No one had asked the identity of his drinking friends. Yet. He knew all about the dangers of becoming intimidated by silence into saying a lot more than was wise. Take the attack into the enemy camp—why not?

'What's all this about, anyhow, Inspector? Has something happened here while I've been away?'

'You could say that.' The man switched his shrewd blue eyes on to full beam. 'The body of a young woman was taken from the sea at Pendrufford Point last night.'

Adrian's heart began to thump. The time had come to get a grip on himself.

'That's terrible. What happened?' He stopped and thought for a moment. 'Wait a minute—wasn't there a lady from there who's been missing from home?'

'You'd heard the story, then?'

Those eyes of his had sharpened into twin points of concentration.

'Yes. I've been going out with a local girl once or twice. She told me about it.'

'Tracey Harman?'

'That's right.'

'It was Tracey Harman's body which was recovered, Mr Sheppard.'

Adrian felt himself swaying; put a hand on the wall for

support. 'Tracey! Good God Almighty! I don't believe it!
Not Tracey!'

'I'm very much afraid it's true. And the post mortem
indicates that her death was no accident.'

'You mean—someone killed her? She was murdered?
Tracey?'

'Yes.'

'The bastard!'

Someone had once told him what happened at post
mortems: first the head, then the body, opened up for
inspection, samples put in jars. He could see that warm,
responsive little body lying on a slab, cold and lifeless.
Adrian retched and headed for the sink, waves of nausea
racking his body.

The two policemen watched; impassive.

He wiped from his eyes the tears brought on by fruitless
vomiting.

'I understand, Mr Sheppard, that you had an appointment to meet Tracey Harman at lunch-time yesterday;
that she took the day off school in order to keep that
appointment?'

'That's right. Here,' he exploded suddenly, 'you're not
suggesting that I had anything to do with this terrible
business, are you? Good Lord, you must be mad! I really
liked that girl!'

The officers exchanged glances.

'I am sure you did, Mr Sheppard. What we'd like is for
you to help establish her movements as clearly as possible
for the time preceding her death.' He glanced out of the
open window at the adjacent caravans. 'It's a bit public
here, though. Might be better if we went back to the
station, and you can make a full statement.'

Adrian could only stare at them, lost for words. He
knew his rights under the law; knew that he was quite at
liberty to refuse to go anywhere, answer any questions,
unless some charge was preferred against him. Even then,

he didn't have to say a word.

'Yes, all right.'

It all sounded so simple, so unthreatening; but Adrian knew that he was going to be asked a great many questions far more searching than any that had been asked so far.

Tracey's mother had never been a prepossessing woman, neither had she ever had a husband of her own. Now her only child was dead. The impact of grief had left her face blotched and hideous as she scrabbled at Susanne's hands.

'I simply had to come and see you, Mrs Hyson,' she said repeatedly.

Even as she found herself drawing back from the implicit suggestion of closer bodily contact, Susanne thought it dreadful that a figure of tragedy should appear so grotesque: lank hair, bad teeth, dirty fingernails, swollen eyes. She had no idea what she should say.

'I'm so glad you did, Mrs Harman.' She sent frantic eye signals across the bowed head; Stan was already on his way, brandy glass in one hand, a box of mansize tissues in the other.

What was there to say to a woman in circumstances like these? All the usual expressions of sympathy seemed cruelly inappropriate.

'I knew you wouldn't mind me coming up here, you being so fond of Tracey. Thought ever such a lot of you, she did, Mrs Hyson. You've no idea what I've been through, no idea at all. Haven't had a wink of sleep ever since they came and told me. To see her lying there like that—'

The weeping grew to a storm of uncontrolled gulps and sobs, great shuddering breaths. Susanne put her arm round the shaking shoulders, began to pat at her hand.

Stan leant forward.

'Mrs Harman, if there is anything at all we can do, you must let us know at once. But you must be desperately tired. Why not let me drive you home to get some rest? Has the doctor given you anything to help you sleep?'

The woman nodded, rooted in her jacket pocket and produced a bottle of pills which she offered for inspection.

'Not that I expect they'll do any good,' she said. 'But at least —' suddenly vicious— 'they've got the bloke that did it.'

Susanne tried to swallow the sudden constriction in her throat. 'They have?'

'Yes. Took him away about an hour ago, they did. That Adrian. Helping the police with their enquiries, but we all know what that really means. I told Tracey over and over again that he was a bad lot, out for what he could get. And when he couldn't get what he wanted —' She smothered her face in a handful of tissues. 'You hear about that sort of thing happening to innocent young girls all the time, but you never think it's going to happen to a child of your own.'

Stan knelt on the carpet beside her, his voice quiet and soothing: 'Let me take you home, Mrs Harman.'

The woman sniffed, consulted her watch and sat up briskly. Mopped her face, pushed her hair back behind her ears and got herself under control.

'Well, yes. That would be kind of you, Mr Hyson. I've got some reporters and photographers coming soon to get my story. They're going to put it in the paper. Might even be on television. So I'd better be on my way. Mind if I use your loo?'

She left the room to an astounded silence.

'My God, I just don't believe it!' Susanne looked stonily at the pile of discarded tissues on the sofa; buried her face in her hands.

Stan touched his finger lightly to her lips and held her close.

★

The police station at Port Laverock was light and modern, a two-storey building with picture windows and rubber tiles in dimpled grey. A wide and formal staircase ended in a spacious reception area bright with potted greenery, polished woodwork and posters about rabies. A notice board open to public inspection invited it to join its community police in the prevention of crime, or to sponsor contenders in a table tennis marathon organized by its own sub-division to raise funds for the local youth club.

The young policeman on the desk glanced up as the CID office door opened and Adrian Sheppard was shown out. Detective-Sergeant Golspie escorted him to the main entrance and held open the swing glass door as he left.

'You're letting him go, then?'

'Yes. For the time being.'

'What d'you reckon, then?'

Sergeant Golspie pursed his narrow lips and drew in a long whistling intake of breath.

'Difficult to say. Seems very shocked; denies passionately that he'd ever laid a finger on the girl. Agrees she went to his caravan lunch-time yesterday, and after a bit of how's your father, gave her a lift to Port Laverock. He was going over to Torbay and wanted her to go with him, but she claimed her mother would never let her go all that way with him. Said he could give her a lift to Port Laverock because there was a record she wanted to buy, and she'd walk back by the coastal path.'

'Easier to come on the school bus, surely?'

'She'd taken the day off school. Probably didn't think too much of that idea.'

'So someone attacked her on the coastal path and threw her off the cliffs that side of Treskellan?'

'Seems that way. The body came in on the tide on the south side of Pendrufford Point. It figures. The Sheppard lad says he went on to Torbay, had a look around, met up with a bunch of lads there and went to a few pubs. We've been able to identify one or two of the pubs; we're checking them out now.'

'But he still could have done it?'

'Oh yes. And so could a lot of other people. The whole place is crawling with visitors for a start. And there's Christopher Quinn. He was with his sister when he found the body, and his own wife hasn't turned up yet. His story about that is a bit dodgy. Very dodgy indeed, in fact.'

'That's Russell Quinn's brother?'

'Yes. Highly respected family around here, the Quinns. But when we checked out that cottage of his at Pendrufford, it was almost clean of any prints at all. Like someone had gone over it. He says Russell Quinn's wife gave the place a good going over last week ready for him and his wife coming down for the summer. Very house-proud lady, Melanie Quinn. At least, that's his story.'

'What d'you reckon, then?' said the young man, for the second time. Again the answer was preceded by that long, indrawn whistle of breath.

'I reckon both of them are hiding something; and neither of them can really account for what they were doing late yesterday afternoon which is when the PM report reckons she must have been killed. Somewhere between five and seven, near enough. Christopher Quinn says he went for a long walk to do some thinking. On his own. Nowhere near that part of the coastal path, of course. The rest of the time he was with his sister Alexis, who supports his story.'

'Well, she would, wouldn't she?'

'But there again, Sheppard has an interesting background. No criminal record, yet, but well known on his own patch. Coming along nicely, they say, as one of the new generation of clever young crooks. The ones with brains. You know who his dad was, don't you?'

The young constable shook his head.

'Jason Sheppard. Before your time. A right villain. Cat burglar. Nothing but the best — silver, jewellery, that sort of thing. Country houses. Posh London flats. Worked alone. No weapons, no aggro. A dying breed, these days.'

'Where is he now, Sergeant?'

'Died in the nick; slipped off a roof somewhere in Berkshire and smashed an ankle, or they'd never have caught him that time either. Must be about ten years ago. Died soon afterwards. Heart attack.'

'And the son takes after him?'

'That's the way it seems. Hasn't been caught yet; too clever for that. And we've no information about any major burglaries in this part of the world, so he may be telling the truth. Only came down here on holiday. The main thing in his favour over the Tracey Harman business is that there's never been any suspicion of violence against him. Takes a pride in using skill and intelligence to get what he wants.'

'Suppose he pushes off — gives us the slip?'

Golspie gave him a tired smile. He never forgot that once he'd been a keen young probationer himself; liked to encourage the youngsters.

'He knows all about Judges' Rules, that one. More than Christopher Quinn does. Sheppard's playing it all very safe and by the book. The decent citizen inadvertently caught up in a very nasty business who is only too anxious to be helpful. But he knows we can't keep him here against his will, so he ups and leaves as soon as he's signed his statement. All very proper.'

'Shame we can't pick him up on a holding charge.'

Golspie eyed his uniformed colleague with suspicion. 'Oh yes? Like what?'

'Well . . .' The young constable began to grow pink of face. 'I was thinking. If Tracey Harman was under age, and the post mortem showed she'd been having it off, that would be an offence, wouldn't it? Or can't you charge people with unlawful sexual intercourse if the — er — young lady isn't alive any more?'

Golspie heaved a despairing sigh.

'Get back to your lost dogs, sonny, and leave the real brain work to the rest of us. I've got work to do.'

During the tourist season the best time for an evening gallop was when the tide was out and after the trippers had all gone home for their evening meal. The dispersal would begin each day around five, when young children grew tired and fretful, their parents short of temper after long hours on the beach. Thermos flasks and polythene containers were piled into baskets, windbreaks dismantled, rugs shaken free of loose sand, and weary fathers would lift toddlers high on to their shoulders for the trek back to car park or caravan, to hotel or guest house. Young mothers, sometimes with grannies, followed behind with pushchairs and bulging bags of swimming gear, beach balls and folding deckchairs. All of them scorched with sunshine, sticky with salt and sand.

Angela usually went riding with Penny Armstrong, whose parents ran the local riding stables, but tonight Penny was too upset over Tracey's death to think of going out for an evening ride.

Which was something of a relief, as Angela badly wanted a chance to think. To think about Tracey, and the way the police had descended on the school to talk to everyone who had known her; about the final school assembly of the year — normally an occasion of great rejoicing — overlaid by a brief but sombre speech by the headmaster, not at all sure how to deal with the situation. As the school had bent its collective head in prayer for Tracey's family and friends, Angela had been upset to find herself wondering what he had done about Tracey's school report. Had he gone round all the staff asking them to write a new one in more charitable vein? A report which might give more lasting comfort to Tracey's mother than the original would have done?

A last gallop along the shore to the far headland, sand and spray spattering on either hand from flying hooves, and it was time to take the pony back to the stables. She felt much better for the ride, more clear-headed. Up over the dunes, trotting quietly now, and across the open moorland thick with gorse and brambles. Quiet and deserted.

The pony shied a little as a streak of golden fur raced towards them out of the bushes. Angela reined in.

'Hello, Jezebel! What are you doing up here, then?' She looked over the landscape falling away to the sea. Not a sign of Susanne or Stan. 'You haven't gone and run away again, have you?' The labrador hung her head. 'You're a naughty girl, Jezebel. You'd better stick with us, and I'll take you back when I go home.'

For a few hundred yards the labrador ran around behind them, sniffing eagerly at each new scent. Then a rabbit shot out of the undergrowth and Jezebel was off in pursuit, straight towards the thicket near the headland.

'Jezebel!' cried Angela in alarm. 'Jezebel. Come back here, you idiot!'

But she was too late. The dog was out of sight when there was a sudden commotion of scrabbling and yelping, followed by a dreadful silence. Then a long-drawn howl of abject misery.

The men from the mine rescue group were calm and cheerful, accustomed to the saving of livestock from mine and cliff falls, from flooded quarries and slurry pits. All four of them jumped down from a big orange lorry standing high off the ground, a crane positioned on its open back. Three of them went straight to the thicket to assess the situation.

The driver nodded towards Mr Armstrong.

'You made the emergency call, sir?'

'Yes. The name's Armstrong, from the stables. We can't thank you enough for coming so quickly. A golden labrador, name of Jezebel; went over into the mineshaft. Oh — this is Angela Quinn, who saw what happened, and her parents.' He lowered his voice. 'I thought it best to get them over too, just in case. The girl's a bit upset. It's been one thing after the other for her just recently.'

The man nodded again; looked kindly at the white-faced girl.

'You did all the right things, milove. Getting help right away without panicking. Good thing you saw it too. Your dog, is it?'

She shook her head.

'No. But I know her. Jezebel belongs to Mr and Mrs Hyson who live next door. D'you think she's going to be all right?'

He laughed. 'From the noise she's making, I reckon she's going to survive. It's the ones that don't make any noise we get worried about. Quite near the top too, from the sound of her.' He raised his eyebrows towards one of the men who had climbed over the barbed wire fencing and was inspecting the crumbling shaft entrance, funnelled from long erosion. The man nodded back at him.

'Yes. She's been lucky. She's on a ledge about twelve feet down.'

Russell let out a sigh of relief; smiled at his wife.

'Thank God for that! We thought it better not to tell the Hysons — the dog's owners — what had happened, just in case she might not be saved. They're devoted to Jezebel.'

'Probably wise,' said the driver. 'The last thing we want is hysterical owners getting under our feet.'

Angela gave a tremulous smile. 'But she could still slip from the ledge? Fall down into the water?'

'Now don't you worry, milove. We'll have her out in no time at all. We get a lot like this, you know; sheep and dogs mostly in a place like this. A dog sets off after a rabbit — well, it's natural isn't it? — and the rabbit swerves off out of danger at right angles, and the poor dog goes straight on.'

'Yes, that's exactly what happened. She didn't even seem to notice the barbed wire fencing — just went right under it.'

'That's the trouble with dogs; they never learnt to read neither. Now you just stay there with your folks, like a good girl.'

He went off to join the resuce party, engaged in laying a protective sheet made from a conveyor belt over the crumbling edge of the shaft. Next they began to unwinch a long coil of anti-twist wire with a triangular space bar attached, all the time calling out reassuring comments to the trapped dog crying dismally from the depths below.

The four observers stood back, watching intently as two of the men, wearing helmets fitted with visors and lamps, were harnessed, one at each end of the bar, before being lowered slowly out of sight into the damp slimy depths of the shaft.

'It looks terribly dangerous,' said Angela. 'Do you really think everything's going to be all right?'

'Yes, darling,' said Melanie, wide-eyed with suspense. 'I'm sure it is. These men are very experienced.'

'But some of the shafts are hundreds of feet deep, and full of water at the bottom. We studied them at school. Supposing Jezebel panics, and slips off the ledge?'

'You mustn't think about it,' said Russell firmly. 'Jezebel is a sociable beast. She'll be delighted to see a friendly face. And your mother's right: these men are experts. I once saw them get a large bullock up a sheer cliff face when it had fallen down on to the shore. But for them it would have drowned when the tide came in.'

The seconds passed like minutes as the rescue went on. The pleasant driver was back in the van, in radio telephonic communication with the men underground. Then the wire began to tighten as the lift began, and there was a shout of triumph as Jezebel, attended by one of the men, emerged into the open, legs dangling from her restraining harness.

Angela clapped her hands and ran forward, half laughing, half crying. Mr Armstrong put out a hand to check her, handed her a dog lead he had been keeping out of sight in his pocket. She thanked him, and ran to where the men were conferring together, freeing the dog and examining her for possible injury.

The driver patted her with affection and smiled up at Angela.

'There you are, milove. What did I tell you? She's a bit mucky and frightened, but she's perfectly safe and sound.'

'Oh thank you! Thank you very much indeed!'

Russell and Melanie had joined the excited group, laughing with relief.

'And now, young Angela,' said the driver, 'why don't you and your mother take Jezebel and wait in your father's car for a moment? Give her a chance to calm down while I have a word with Mr Armstrong.'

As he watched them go, the driver's smile vanished.

'Didn't like to say anything in front of the little girl, but you'd better get the police up here right away.'

Russell was seized by a terrible premonition.

'The police?'

'Yes. There's something else down that mineshaft, the lads tell me. Floating in the water a long way down. They think it's a body.'

CHAPTER 8. THURSDAY

During the night the weather changed. By morning great banks of mist had rolled in from the Atlantic to smother the village in a thick blanket of white candyfloss. And with it came the first waves of pervasive fear, seeping silently into every household: a malignant fear not readily dispersed.

For those who had known Caroline Quinn it seemed fitting that the sun should cease to shine, that the elements should conspire to muffle the coast in mourning. There were few who had not heard just what had been raised from the mineshaft the night before, or that it would have been impossible for her to have fallen there by chance. First Tracey, now Caroline.

There had to be some maniac at large.

Susanne was not the only one to feel a disturbing relief that the uncertainty was over: a relief which vanished at the realization that an even more terrible uncertainty was about to begin. She had considered closing down the salon for the day as a mark of respect. Treskellan folk by tradition showed great respect for their dead, but this was no ordinary death in the sense of a life drawing naturally to its close. Better, perhaps, to try to carry on as normal. Normal? Nothing, she thought, was ever going to be normal again.

She took the path down to the shore, oblivious of her surroundings, looking only at the ground as step followed step through the bushes. Already she could imagine what would happen directly she opened for business: the succession of clients with only one topic on their minds: curious, fearful, insinuating according to temperament. The bad weather would have meant an increase in passing trade at any time; now she would be invaded by every sensation-seeker from miles around. Every woman knew that Susanne's would become the focal point of village interest and gossip.

At the foot of the path she glanced at the windows of Shrimp Cottage. Curtains drawn. Another mark of respect? She turned left along Fore Street. So long as Melanie stayed away, Susanne felt she could cope. She could survive by refusing to become involved in any discussion other than the usual parochial topics of health and weather, lest she be lured into saying more than was wise. To act naturally, she was finding, was the most difficult thing in the world. And if frightened people needed to talk, they could do it somewhere else. There would be no idle gossip today of maniacs or any other theory; especially the one—as yet unvoiced—that Christopher Quinn was in it up to his neck.

Melanie was sure to want to stay with her family, after all they had been through. Surely.

Susanne was wrong. Melanie was standing in the doorway rubbing droplets of moisture from her hair. Her face looked crumpled, as though she had aged ten years overnight. Susanne felt an unexpected surge of pleasure and affection to see her waiting there. She should have known better. In times of crisis the Melanies of this world came into their own; loyal, capable, prepared to handle any emergency the good Lord might choose to send.

'What a change in the weather!' remarked Melanie abruptly. 'How's Jezebel?'

Susanne felt tears spring to her eyes, and brushed them away as she bent to unlock the door. That this overwrought, undemanding woman could even think of Jezebel at a time like this moved her deeply.

'She's just fine, thanks. None the worse for her adventure. We'll always be grateful to Angela for what she did.'

'Yes.' Melanie followed her into the shop. 'It's an ill wind, I suppose.'

Susanne swallowed, not at all sure whether Melanie wanted, needed to talk. Was there anything at all one could say? She was saved by Geoff putting his head round the doorway, eyes heavy with lack of sleep, but bouncy of step. He drew up smartly when he saw Melanie.

'Ah,' he began, quickly rephrasing what he had been about to say. ' 'Morning, Melanie. How are you, love?'

She gave him a tired smile.

'I'll be fine, just so long as no one comes in saying how sorry they are. I'd be quite liable to hit them.'

Susanne moved quietly to the reception desk as Geoff laughed.

'Attagirl! That's the spirit. You can cope with anything except sympathy. Just popped in to say we've got Alex and Chris to sleep at last. Took us nearly all night, after the excitement was all over. Wore them out with non-stop talking, like a wake, you know. Splendid idea, wakes. Very therapeutic. Better than all that furious control your family goes in for. Together with a bit of the hard stuff. They're both out like lights at the moment, with Toby standing guard.'

Melanie squeezed his arm.

'You're a good friend, Geoff. Don't think we don't know this is pretty dreadful for you too, you know.'

He held up a warning hand.

'Now don't start that, or you'll have me blubbing down your nice pinny. Russell gone off to work as well?'

'Yes. Of course he's a bit short on sleep too, but there are arrangements to be made—inquests and funerals, all that side of things. Better if he's on the spot in Port Laverock to do all that with the police. Can't really expect Chris to do it all.'

Susanne looked up from the appointments diary.

'What about Angela? I thought school had finished?'

'That's right. I let her sleep in. She'll be going over to the stables later on. Mrs Armstrong said last night she could have her lunch there.'

'But is that wise?'

'It seemed a good idea to me — get her away for the day.'

'But —' Susanne glanced across at Geoff — 'I don't want to sound alarmist, but should she really be left on her own? I mean, if there really is some maniac around. And it does rather seem that there might be, don't you think?'

Melanie turned white.

'Dear God, you're right. And I've left her all alone in the house! I'm just not thinking straight at all. I was so busy thinking that it must have been Adrian who —' She broke off. 'It still could, I suppose. Be Adrian, I mean. He may be one of those psychopaths we're always hearing about. I'd better go straight back.'

Susanne picked up the phone.

'Calm down, Melanie. I'll ring Stan and get him to go and stay in the house till she's ready. Then he can drive her over to the stables.'

Melanie watched her dial. 'There was a full moon that night, you know,' she said darkly.

'What night?'

'The night Caroline's car was seen down here. Last Friday.'

Geoff frowned and began to fidget as Susanne talked with her husband. When she'd finished:

'I think I'll just pop up to The Shrubberies as well,' he said. 'One or two things I'd like to talk over with Stan.'

Susanne watched him disappear into the mist, her eyes narrowed and thoughtful.

Lunch-time; Stan at the cooker making a quick omelette.

'All right, Sue?'

She nodded, buried her face in Jezebel's coat.

'It's been a madhouse. We've sold more tights and shampoo in a morning than I've done since we opened. Mostly tourists, come to gawp at Melanie. Notoriety by association. Then they can go back home and regale their friends with a good story. It makes you sick. Geoff and Toby are doing sentry duty defending Shrimp Cottage against all comers. Photographers everywhere, amateur and professional. Thank God the mist hasn't lifted — their shots should be nicely ruined. Chris went off with the police about half an hour ago, looking like a zombie. There's Tracey's inquest as well, so Alex has to go too. Toby's taking her this afternoon. Those two haven't had a lot of sleep either.'

Stan handed her an omelette, a green salad.

'I shall stand over you until you eat it, you know.'

She picked up a fork.

'Stan, what did Geoff want? To talk to you about, I mean?'

'Not a lot. Just keeping in touch, I think. Why do you ask?'

'I've got a nasty feeling, Stan, that Geoff is becoming rather suspicious.'

'Suspicious of whom? Everyone in general, or me in particular?'

She sighed: 'I only wish I knew.'

Toby lay dozing in an armchair, lulled into semi-consciousness by driving rain drumming against the window. He would have given much to be able to go upstairs to bed, but Geoff was still prowling aimlessly round the room.

'Why don't you try to get some rest, Geoff? We're all exhausted, and there's nothing we can do any more.'

Geoff glared down at him.

'Don't be stupid. We've only got thirty-six hours left.'

'For what?'

'Oh God, use your brains. We have to go home after that.'

'So? You don't imagine it's going to make a lot of difference whether we're here or not?' Toby tried to inject a conciliatory note into his voice. 'Look, I do understand something of what you must be feeling, but the police must know what they're doing. All we can do now is wait.'

Geoff threw himself on the couch.

'Wait!' he said savagely. 'For God's sake! It seems to me that the police have damn-all to go on: Tracey half-throttled and thrown off a cliff, Caroline strangled and dumped down a mineshaft. End of story.' He plucked at the frayed upholstery on the couch, rolling small pieces of fluff between his fingers. 'There has to be some motive behind it all. Why should anyone want to kill Caroline? Or Tracey, come to that?' He cleared his throat, glanced across with speculation in his eyes. 'It really sounds as though it has to be one of us, don't you think?'

For a few seconds Toby studied the cuticles of his fingernails; began to push them back.

'Look, Geoff, why not leave well alone? We can't sit here doing a vivisection act on people we know. It's not decent.'

'So you've had the same idea?'

'Well—not necessarily.' He bit at the skin of his left thumbnail. 'It may well have been some total stranger—someone down here on holiday who went berserk, or something. And there's Adrian Sheppard. He was here last week when Caroline went missing.'

'That would be very convenient, wouldn't it?' Geoff's expression was grim. 'Melanie was muttering ominous things about moon madness this morning; said it was full moon the night Caroline died. It was too. I checked. Perhaps some madman struck that night, and got a taste for it. Had a go at Tracey four nights later.'

'Do we know for sure that Caroline was killed on Friday?'

'Not really. But that was the night the anonymous phone caller said her car was seen here, and no one's reported seeing her alive since.'

'If only we knew who made that call. A man, Chris says, with no particular accent, but plenty of people here don't have local accents. It might have been a hoax, of course, or Chris made the story up himself.'

'Possible, but unlikely. After all, she was found down here.'

Toby rubbed his eyes, dragged himself from his chair.

'It may sound unfeeling, but I'm starving. Could you go a few rounds of toasted cheese?'

Geoff looked up, surprised. 'You know, I could really fancy that. Thought this morning I'd never want to eat again. But keep right on talking. I'm so confused I can't think straight. Luckily, you've got one of those nice orderly minds, and it's not as though you're really one of us. It's much easier for you.'

Toby felt a sharp stab of resentment, of jealousy; looked at Geoff's tortured face and tried to make allowances. Again he wondered about the nature of the relationship between Geoff and Caroline.

'It seems incredible,' said Geoff after a long silence, 'that one of us might be a killer.'

Toby was strongly inclined to resist the probing. He piled up slices of brown bread, began to saw great slabs of Cheddar cheese. Made his decision.

'Yes. I'm afraid I can't subscribe to the maniac theory.'

'So freelance psychopaths are out?'

'Unless—' Toby chose his words with care— 'we are nurturing our own friendly psychopath without realizing it. One of the over-controlled breed. You know, where friends and relations end up saying they just can't believe it—he was always such a nice quiet helpful chap.'

'My God — I never thought of that! A motiveless killer?'

'Something like that. A twisted motive, not like the usual run of murders and assaults which are so often committed by someone the victim already knows quite well: like a member of the family.' He glanced out of the corner of his eye at Geoff but went on slicing tomatoes with careful precision.

'On the other hand,' he went on casually, 'Tracey may have died because of something she'd seen, or heard, or even just suspected, which ensured that she had to be silenced. She was quite a sharp, inquisitive youngster, and I'd think she could be quite spiteful, from what I saw of her. I'm sorry, Geoff. I know you liked her, but you did ask for the outsider's point of view.'

'Just pretend I haven't any sensibilities, and we'll get on much better. I'm only after the truth.'

'Fine.' He lit the grill. 'I don't know enough about Caroline even to hazard a motive; but I'm afraid an outsider would be pretty suspicious of Christopher's account of what happened at the London end. If he's telling the truth, I doubt if it's the whole truth. It would be interesting to know what it is he's hiding. Something quite trivial, perhaps. There may have been a row which he's far too much of a gentleman to talk about, and Caroline packed her bags and came down here. From what I've heard about her, that would seem quite in character. Maybe Melanie was right, and she set off to meet some man friend. Or she may have come to Treskellan to meet someone: someone who phoned her, or sent her a message, and who may have ended up killing her.'

Geoff remained silent. Toby pushed a fish slice under a bubbling piece of toasted cheese and put it on a plate.

'Again,' he went on, 'she may never have got here alive in the first place. She could have been killed in London, or Bournemouth, or anywhere in between, and her body driven down. By someone who knew the district well enough to know where there was a convenient mineshaft, and then drove back to London in her car.'

Geoff looked thoughtful. 'So we're back to Chris again?'

'Except that the case against Chris tends to fall apart because of the time factor. I just don't think it could be done.'

'Thank God for that!'

'Which leaves two further options.' He picked up two plates piled high with toasted cheese. 'Someone could be trying to put the poison in for Chris, or he was working in league with a third party.'

'Yes,' said Geoff softly, 'that had occurred to me too, I'm afraid. I just didn't want to think about it.' He watched Toby come back from the kitchen. 'One of the family — Russell or Alex, or even Melanie?' He ran his hands roughly through his hair. 'But it's crazy even to think of it!'

Toby shrugged; handed him his plate. 'Get these inside you.'

For several minutes the two men ate in silence, engaged in their own thoughts and fears. Then Geoff gave a twisted smile.

'Can you see Russell as a killer? Or Alex? The thing's ridiculous.'

'Yes. But there's something about the entire Quinn family. Very controlled bunch. The Hysons too. That old-fashioned characteristic of well-bred people. Very warm and friendly but the sort who will only allow you so far into their emotions, their private lives. Then they hang out a polite signal telling you to keep off the grass, and promptly close ranks.'

'That's true. They've always been like that. All of them. Caroline too. An unseen demarcation line between friendship and familiarity. I wish there were more of it around. But you don't fancy Russell as a suspect?'

Toby shook his head.

'What a question! He's a very likeable man. In another ten years he might be a bit overwhelming; all that camaraderie and threat of backslapping. I think he has a real need to be popular, and it shows. I should think he's a lot less self-confident than he likes to make out.'

Geoff grinned. 'You're developing a nice line in hatchet jobs. I think a lot of Russell. He's been a good friend to me over the years. There were times I thought he should have married Caroline, if he'd met her in time. She's very much — she was very much — into social success as well. Whereas Melanie isn't — not really. All she's ever wanted was to please Russell. A dreadful waste. She's much too intelligent to submerge her personality the way she does. Like an iceberg, seven-eighths out of sight.'

Toby considered Melanie Quinn.

'Does it matter, if she's happy?'

Geoff wiped his mouth on the back of his hand.

'Adoring someone doesn't always mean you're happy. I can imagine Melanie on her knees every night praying the good Lord not to snatch it all away from her. She must be going through hell. She probably believes it was Chris, but won't even allow herself to think it. Loyalty, thy name is Melanie.'

'But I thought you said she suspected Adrian?'

'Well, she would, wouldn't she? She has to go on believing what she wants to believe. She's got a nice nature.' He glanced up. 'I notice you aren't prepared to carry out a character assassination on Alex?'

Toby shifted in his seat.

'I've seen so little of her.' Geoff raised his eyebrows doubtfully. 'Oh, all right, so I'm making excuses. I simply cannot see her involved in any way in this horrendous business.'

'You could try.'

Toby rested his head wearily back against the chair.

'Well, it's obvious she's very attached to her brothers,

Chris especially, but that's only to be expected in the circumstances. And she does know the district like the back of her hand. And she can drive.' He looked up angrily. 'What else do you want me to say?'

'Alex didn't like Caroline too much.'

'Yes, you said. That doesn't mean she killed her, for God's sake!'

Geoff laughed unpleasantly. 'Whatever happened to that objective viewpoint of yours? Fair enough — we'll take it as read that Alex is above suspicion. For the moment.' He yawned. 'Pity the child has such a brother fixation. Not just with the two she's got, but with the male sex in general. She's twenty-three years old, and never had a serious boy-friend that I know about. Just surrogate brothers. Like me, even Stan, who must be twice her age. If you're not very careful, young Toby, you'll end up becoming another one.'

Toby stood up. 'I think,' he said coldly, 'you have a singularly unpleasant mind.'

'Now who's over-reacting? Good God man, surely you realize that in many ways Alex is still a child? She likes things that way. Unawakened, if you want to be poetic. If I were you, I'd get in there fast and get started on a bit of awakening. And wipe that look of outraged piety off your face.'

Toby sat down again.

'Sorry.' His tone was grudging. 'I'm rather fond of Alex.'

'Then get in there fast and tell her so, you young fool!'

'At a time like this? Don't be ridiculous.'

'It's probably just what she needs. You haven't got a lot of time left either.' Geoff looked thoughtful. 'Unless — I could always phone Sheila's mum and ask her to hold the fort for an extra day. Then we could stay on till Sunday. Melanie would put us up for one night.'

'We can't possibly impose on her like that!'

'Of course we can. Don't you want to know how it all ends? Wouldn't you like to spend just one evening alone with Alex?'

'Well—'

'Splendid. I thought for a moment your high moral principles were going to triumph over your morbid curiosity. Melanie wouldn't dream of letting us camp out on the beach.'

'It wouldn't be right to take advantage of her kindness. Why not ask the Hysons?'

'Hardly. I only met them last week. And Melanie would be very offended. Mind you,' he conceded, 'if all else fails, we could try for Goldenacre. It might be fun to get to know them better. Have you noticed how they never talk about themselves at all, or where they came from? Filthy rich, of course. Stan married late, retired early, that's all we know. Can't quite make him out. Self-effacing but no fool; would make a good poker-player. Susanne too—a gorgeous girl—but there's something a bit edgy about her. Looks to Stan quite often as though she wants guidance or approval.'

'So she's in love? Or married out of her class? Anxious about her role as chatelaine of Goldenacre?'

'What a snob you are, young Toby. I suppose they should be on our suspect list too, though I can't imagine how they could be involved in—in what happened to Caroline.' A great sadness filled his eyes. 'Or to Tracey,' he added. An afterthought.

Toby looked at him anxiously.

'As you say—a very controlled lot, our suspects. Look, the rain's stopped. Let's go out and get a breath of fresh air.'

Geoff stood up and stretched.

'It hasn't escaped me, Toby, the delicacy with which you've avoided any reference to the seventh suspect.'

'What seventh?'

'Don't pretend it hasn't crossed your mind that I could have been the person Caroline came down here to meet? Her very close friend alone on his annual break from a life of celibacy? For all you know, Caroline and I might have been a lot more than just good friends.'

'Yes,' admitted Toby unhappily. 'Since you ask, yes, it had occurred to me.'

'And that I might have been feeding you a load of false information all week?'

'Yes. That too.'

'Good. There's just one thing wrong with that hypothesis. Caroline wasn't like that.'

Toby zipped up his jacket.

'And you?'

It was a brutal question: one he should never have asked. But Geoff only smiled.

'Who knows?' he said quietly. 'It was never put to the test.'

There was a staccato knocking at the door and Alex came in, pale and tired but clearly excited.

'Can I come in? I'm not interrupting anything?'

'Not a thing,' said Geoff. 'You're just in time to witness the end of a beautiful friendship.'

'So soon?'

'We've been playing detectives.'

'Haven't we all? Who's your choice?'

'Front runner is Chris, with Stan as the unknown outsider in with a chance.'

Toby flinched, but Alex just raised her eyebrows.

'Stan? We didn't really consider him. We rather thought it might be you, Geoff.'

Geoff's mouth began to open. He closed it again. A muscle twitched at the corner of one eye.

'Well, thank you very much,' he said after a pause. 'It's nice to know who your friends are.'

Alex laughed happily. 'But it wasn't you at all. It was Adrian!'

Toby said sharply. 'He's been charged?'

'I expect so. Chris and I were in Port Laverock waiting for Russell to bring us back from the inquest — it was adjourned like you said it would be, Toby — and we saw a police car heading for the station with him in the back. That's the third time they've had him in, so they must be pretty certain.'

'But you don't know that he's been charged?' persisted Toby.

'What does it matter when they charge him?' asked Alex impatiently. 'What really matters is that we know it wasn't Chris, like half the village was saying. And Melanie was right all the time. She usually is, of course. I thought we might go up to Goldenacre and tell Susanne. Plan some sort of quiet celebration.'

Geoff looked grave. Turned to Toby in some alarm, looked back at the bright-eyed Alex and shook his head.

'No. Alex, I shouldn't do that. Not yet. Not yet, my love.'

She looked up at him, finger to lip. Toby realized in that gesture how deeply shocked and confused the girl was. Longed to put his arms round her and give her comfort.

'Dear Geoff,' she said with a tight little smile, 'you're right, of course. It's just that — I'm so glad for Chris. The police have been giving him a terrible time.'

Toby followed them out into the road, steaming now as the sun emerged from behind the rainclouds. Everything smelt deliciously clean and fresh. Symbolic, perhaps? He frowned. Why on earth should Adrian have killed Caroline?

Outside Goldenacre Geoffrey stopped.

'I think, Alex, it would be best for you to go in on your

own. We'll wait here. Tell them quietly. Caroline is dead, remember; so is Tracey.'

'Yes, of course. But it wasn't Chris. Isn't that enough for a tiny little bit of rejoicing?'

'No, it's not. Not yet. Off you go.'

He was too late. Susanne had seen them from the garden and was coming to meet them. Alex ran forward.

'It's all over, Susanne. We thought we'd let you know. The police know now that it wasn't Chris.'

'Oh Alex, I'm so glad; glad for all of you.' Her brows crinkled. 'But how do you know? What's happened?'

'The police have arrested Adrian Sheppard. I know it sounds terrible, but it's such a relief!'

Toby watched the colour drain from Susanne's face.

'The police have arrested *Adrian*? For *murder*?'

'That's what it looks like,' said Alex happily.

Susanne's lips tightened.

'And that pleases you, I suppose?' She spoke slowly, tiny splashes of pink staining her cheeks. 'Your brother is off the hook, and that's all that concerns you, I suppose. Anyone would think you had a total monopoly on sisterly affection!'

Geoff sprang forward, took her by the arm.

'I shouldn't say any more, Susanne. Not now. Here, let me take you back to Stan.'

As he led her away Alex looked up at Toby. She shivered.

'I was wrong,' she said in a shocked whisper. 'It's not all over yet, is it?'

CHAPTER 9. FRIDAY

Stanley Hyson was a troubled man. He knelt at the open bedroom window drinking in the cool night air. In the distance he could hear the sea, the timeless and incessant surge of waves over sand and shingle, a perpetual backcloth to all the other muted noises of the night.

A car swept through the village, throwing cones of yellow lamplight before it, and was gone. Moths fluttered up and down the window panes and would not go away.

Behind him Susanne's breathing was now soft and regular. Thank God.

Every single day they had lived together Stan had given thanks for the constant joy he found in her presence. He could still hardly believe in the happiness she had brought him, so late in life. There had been no need for that vow that he would cherish her, endow her with all his worldly goods. He had to work at controlling his urge to give her everything she might want, to protect her from every hurt and misfortune.

That she had fallen in love with him at all amazed and bewildered him. Not as a father figure, as he might have expected, but as a man. He was terrified that he might one day inspire in her feelings of gratitude, for gratitude was the most destructive of all emotions: a cold and fleeting thing, a precursor of that sense of obligation which breeds resentment and dislike.

And yet . . .

It seemed that now he had no choice. The time had come for Sue to be protected. No longer could he bear to stand aside and watch her suffer on his account. But if he took control of the situation before it was too late, would that be the greatest insult of all? The proof that he had perceived her as an inferior creature, and so diminished her by that perception?

Susanne was an individual, with a right to her own identity. He could not protect her. He must allow her the freedom to suffer. Or risk that he lose her.

A light-switch clicked.

'That was a very heartfelt sigh. What great conclusion had you reached?'

He turned. Susanne lay back on the pillow, hair tousled, amusement lurking in her eyes.

'I've been lying here watching you for ages.'

An enormous furry moth shot past his head and zoomed in on the light-bulb. Stan chased it round the room and finally captured it; dropped it back outside and closed the window.

'I think I've just discovered how much I need you.'

She smiled. 'That's not new. You're always saying that.'

'No — I've just discovered how much. That's different. Enough to let you go free, if you ever want to. Or have to.'

'That's a whole lot of love, Stan.'

He sat on the bed beside her. 'That's right.'

'Can you tell me about it? What you've been thinking?'

He climbed into bed beside her, and in the warm, safe security of her arms, he talked. He talked about Tracey and Caroline and Adrian, about Geoffrey and Russell and Melanie, about Alex and Chris. He spoke of the dangers that lurked ahead, and the distress and disruption they might bring. He told her that their way of life might never be the same again; that there might be some who might be unable to go on living in the village in the future.

And as he spoke, Susanne's fingers stroked the nape of his neck, as one soothes a child.

'And you think it could be us? We might have to go?'

'Would you mind very much?'

'Yes,' she said. 'I should mind terribly. But so long as

we have one another—'

'We may not even be together, Sue.'

It was out in the open: the biggest truth of all.

'Yes, Stan. I know that. I've always known it. I just went on believing it could never happen. Until now. We're going to have to be very careful.'

'Yes.'

'What about Adrian?'

'Adrian,' said Stan, 'can look after himself.'

A remark, Susanne realized, heavy with ambiguity.

'I expect you're right.' She gave a little sigh and switched out the bedside lamp. 'Stan, I know it's stupid, but would you mind closing the curtains? Then we can shut out the night and pretend we're not afraid.'

The interview room was a good deal more modern than others he had known. Stark and sparsely furnished, but clinically clean, as yet untainted by the lingering smell of sweat and fear.

Adrian stared at the young policeman standing with his back against the wall, beside the door, carefully avoiding any suggestion of eye contact. Both of them waiting for the next development.

Detective-Inspector Bracken had proved to be one of that West Country breed of policeman skilled in combining charm and courtesy with a persistence which was at times unnerving. Adrian had done his best to match him in courtesy and willingness to help. He quite understood that he and his sergeant had a duty to question him with the utmost rigour about his movements, and would do his best to remember every tiny detail of his holiday activities, no matter how long it took.

It had taken a long time—ever since yesterday afternoon. Much longer than it had taken them to discover who his father had been, and check up on his background. It was evident that they would become even more persistent after that.

Yes, he did have a flat of his own near Regents Park. Yes, he had been educated at boarding-school. And yes, his father had set up a trust fund for him which his auntie had drawn on after he died.

And what did he do for a living now? Oh, a bit of dabbling in used cars, a bit of dealing; spent a fair bit of time at the races. Been quite lucky on the tote. No, he hadn't done badly at all, for a youngster. Not that he could quite see what all this had to do with the matter in hand. Perhaps there was nothing more they wished to ask him?

But there was. Back over the old ground: especially to the Friday afternoon when he'd met Tracey off the school bus, gone home for a meal afterwards, then taken a boat out night fishing. They could check with the bloke he'd hired it from. Name of Charlie. Had a blackboard down on the quay where people signed up if they wanted a hire.

They had checked.

Certainly he'd got back late. Very late. He'd never denied it. Beautiful night. Full moon, it was. Yes, he could describe his catch. Certainly he wouldn't mind telling them all over again. Perhaps he should have kept them in the fridge all week if he'd had any idea they might become vital evidence.

He had seen Sergeant Golspie's lips twitch for a moment, and was glad of the warning. This was no time to get smart. And so it went on, an hour by hour account of where he had been, what he had done, right through until the Tuesday night when Tracey's body had been taken from the sea at Pendrufford Point.

Tell us again about the lads you were with at Torquay. Describe them. What were their names? Ever seen any of them before? Wasn't it a little odd, Mr Sheppard, that a bright lad like you seems to remember so little about them? No, Mr Sheppard, we find it hard to believe you were as drunk as all that.

When the going got really tough, he reminded himself of what his father used to say: that the burden of proof lies firmly on the prosecution. No one ever had to prove his innocence. No one was required to say a word in his own defence, and should never talk unless he was very sure what he was doing. Adrian felt he knew exactly what he was doing.

A small squeak from the top hinge, and the door opened. The young constable stiffened as Detective-Inspector Bracken came in, Detective-Sergeant Golspie behind him. Their pleasant smiles gave little indication of the tired frustration both men were feeling that they could no longer justify holding this slippery young man.

Bracken's approach was brisk and businesslike.

'Right, Mr Sheppard. Thank you for helping us with our enquiries.'

'You mean there is nothing more I can do?'

'Not at the moment, thank you.'

Adrian stood up; hesitated. Bracken had been very decent to him, and had a rotten job on his hands. It couldn't do any harm to tell him now.

'Look,' he heard his own voice saying, 'there is something else I should have told you.'

'Yes, Mr Sheppard?'

'Only I thought it might make you think —' He broke off. 'That phone call. To Mr Quinn, up in London. On Monday night.'

Neither officer moved, smiles of encouragement welded across their faces.

'That was me. Tracey and me. Only I did the phoning in case he recognized her voice and we got mixed up in it all. We'd seen a red Fiat going down to Pendrufford Point on Friday night, and Tracey got really worried when she heard that Mr Quinn's wife was missing up in London. I

know I should have told you before, but when you're
being questioned all the time, it makes you a bit nervous.'

Bracken's smile melted.

'Sit down, Mr Sheppard. Perhaps you'd like to make
another statement?'

Russell stubbed out a cigarette with such force that the
filter tip broke off. He looked with distaste at the ash on
his fingertips, the contents of the heavy cut-glass ashtray.
That must have been his seventh since arriving at the
office. Melanie was right — he really must try to cut it
down. Not yet, though. Not now.

He caught his breath in that irritating cough he'd
developed recently, and sipped at the dregs of his coffee.
It tasted cold and revolting, but at least it was served on a
tray with fine bone china and a plate of biscuits. One of
the few visible privileges accorded to the rank of General
Manager.

His personal offices had never been as imposing as he
would have liked, but the old family firm of Cranston's
was firmly rooted in the Wesleyan tradition of thrift and
industry, imbued with the principles of fear in the Lord
and care of its employees in almost equal measure.
Patriarchal, almost feudal, it had grown from the tiny
draper's shop of Victorian times into one of the finest
departmental stores in the West, still adhering to the
tenets of service and gentility on which it had been
founded.

An anachronism really, at a time when hypermarkets
and self-service chain stores had sent so many small busi-
nesses into bankruptcy. But Cranston's had survived the
challenge, largely due to the business flair and enthusiasm
Russell had brought to the firm. He had joined them
straight from College, and risen steadily to his present
position. There he had planned to stay, never likely to
make the board of governors: his only unfulfilled ambition.

Cranston's was essentially a family firm, and that sort of power remained vested among the members of the family.

It was in the spring that rumours of impending change first began to circulate. The two surviving members of the older generation were now in their seventies; the younger generation, it was said, could hardly wait to realize its shares by selling out to one of the national multiples. Ominous mutterings of drastic change, the shadow of redundancies, were heard. The whole of Russell's personal security was being threatened.

He put his elbows on the desk and rested his chin on clenched fists. Reached out for a cigarette and lit it. He had heard of this sort of thing happening to others at the peak of their careers. And the timing could not possibly have been worse. He knew he was a popular and respected member of the community, both in Port Laverock and at home. He had a generous income, total control within his province, annual bonuses. A brand-new house, a wonderful wife and a beautiful daughter. His face softened as it always did when he thought of Angela these days. She was bright and intelligent, and he had discovered that very special relationship between a father and growing daughter which had surprised him. His only child. She was going to have the very best of everything love and money could provide.

They had just moved into The Shrubberies when the local grapevine produced the first hard rumours of a coming takeover. At once he had altered all his immediate plans; taken precautions to safeguard his position. In a strange way it had been exciting, taking up a new and absorbing challenge. At the start, all had gone well. His natural business acumen, his ability to think ahead, to predict with clarity, had been to his advantage.

Then his luck began to run out.

Russell went over to the steel filing cabinet and extracted

a bottle half full of scotch from the bottom drawer. Poured himself out a decent measure and sipped it slowly. Went back to his desk and picked up yet again the letter at the top of his in-tray. Typewritten, with an imposing letterhead; informing him that, on the instructions of the owners, representatives from a firm of accountants wished to make an early appointment in anticipation of a proposed merger.

He was upset and hurt. They might have told him. He had enough on his mind at the moment without that as well. He was finding he could no longer keep the separate parts of his life—work, family, church, leisure—in neat individual compartments; nor keep his mind on any single issue for any length of time.

He bowed his head, drummed his fingers on the desk. Time was what he needed, and time was running out fast. Time to think, to plan, to act.

Tonight! It was Friday. Late night opening on Fridays had been one of his more successful innovations, a duty he shared with his assistant. Tonight would be his turn. He'd put a DO NOT DISTURB notice on the door, and get to work then.

A trim young lady put her head round the door.

'Yes, Hilary?'

'You've got a visitor, Mr Quinn.' She lowered her voice. 'I don't know who he is, but he says you'd want to see him. A Mr Adrian Sheppard.'

Russell's pulse began to race. He reached for a cigarette, realized he was already smoking; kept his voice cool. cool.

'Yes, that's all right, Hilary. Show Mr Sheppard in, will you?'

Both men waited until the door had closed behind the girl.

'And about time too!' said Russell with venom. 'Do you realize what a ghastly mess you've got us into?'

★

Five minutes' walk from the police station was a dark, old-fashioned pub where Detective-Inspector Bracken would have a lunch-time pint and pasty in peace whenever he got the chance. He carried them over to a seat in the corner and settled back to think again about the case of Caroline Quinn.

In a country division where neighbourly gossip was a growth industry, it was frustrating that so little hard information had emerged from endless hours of enquiry. Symptomatic of the tourist season, when hosts of visitors might come and go, wander and explore at all hours without remark. The locals had no real interest in what they got up to as wave succeeded wave all through the summer.

Visitors like Adrian Sheppard. Residents on caravan sites probably aroused less interest than any others, except from those who shared the site. Even they tended to be out all day, but Adrian's neighbours had so far confirmed those parts of his story which they had observed. Bracken would like to know much more about that young man. No form as yet, but as he'd said himself, he'd been lucky. The last person to have been seen with Tracey, his movements after that completely without corroboration.

Nor was Sheppard the only person immediately concerned in this enquiry about whom he knew little. There were the new people up at Goldenacre, the Hysons, already admitted to the bosom of the close-knit Quinn family. Which was rather remarkable in itself, really, when Goldenacre had been the ancestral family home. A reserved couple, not at all forthcoming about anything not directly connected with the matters in hand. Shrewd sort of chap; his wife an attractive young woman who'd kept her distance, answered questions with marked hesitation once or twice. Ran the hairdresser's shop where she employed Melanie Quinn. She'd employed Tracey Harman too.

There could be something there.

Then there was the golden labrador, Jezebel, who had led them to the discovery of Caroline Quinn's body. A lovely beast, well cared for. How did she come to be running loose that evening? Returning to familiar ground? Had she been there a few days earlier, perhaps shut up in a car while one—or both—of her owners had been engaged in getting rid of the body? There had been no tyre marks nearby, but there had been no rain for weeks, and the ground was rock hard.

Bracken was a local man who had known Russell Quinn all his life. In recent years he had lost touch with the others, with Chris and Caroline living in London, Alex away at college. Melanie, of course, he knew by sight — she was often in Port Laverock shopping. A bit on the dowdy side but a really kind woman, by all accounts. Apparently as committed to the family welfare as any of the blood-related Quinns.

They'd all been distraught and anxious to help. Except for Christopher, of course. Been very cagey, had Christopher. Bracken sighed. There walked the prime suspect, could one but find a motive, an opportunity. Hedged around, protected by a small army of loyal family and friends.

Still, they had all accounted freely for their movements during the crucial times: at work, on the golf-course, seeing friends. Where possible, these had been checked. It was the hours spent at home, in the garden, out walking, which were suspect in that corroboration had come over-whelmingly from one another. Which of them would be loyal enough to fabricate an alibi, substantiate a false one? Which of them, apart from Chris, might have a motive for killing Caroline?

Geoff Taverner now, staying at the holiday cottage in the village, next door to Alex. Been coming down for years and known—since that rotten accident to his wife — to have become very friendly with Caroline Quinn. And Toby Wilde, who'd been a student once with Alex, arriving in Port Laverock the day before Caroline went missing. Melanie had prevented him from coming to Treskellan until the Saturday. Curious, that. Had he really stayed away from his girl-friend during those two days, or had he paid a private visit to the village which was not common knowledge?

Bracken pushed back his plate and stared into the middle distance. Far too many charming, pleasant and helpful individuals. He must guard against dangerous pre-conceptions. Bracken had known a great many charming and pleasant villains in his time.

Think again of the victims: Tracey Harman, only fifteen, still a child. It was fortunate, in the interests of truth, that she had been at school with his own children. Bracken had heard of Tracey's reputation long before her horrifying death had exerted its censorship on people's memories. Pert, precocious, prying, Tracey might well have invited the sort of attention which brought about her death.

But Caroline Quinn presented a very different proposition: a mature woman, lively, imperious, well able to look after herself. She, too, had met with a horrible death.

With Caroline, his thoughts had come full circle, back to the central issue of what she had been doing in Treskellan at all on Friday night. In solving that question, Bracken felt sure he would discover the key to the tragedies. Someone in the village knew the answer; of that he was convinced.

Unless the sensation-mongers were right, and there was some lunatic loose among them. It was not a theory he favoured himself, and there had been no forensic evidence to support it. A more sinister thought was that he might be dealing with two quite separate crimes.

Detective-Sergeant Golspie pushed his way through the throng of people round the bar.

'Thought you might be here. I followed Sheppard, like you said. Guess where he went?'

Bracken looked up sourly:

'Suppose you tell me.'

'Straight to Cranston's. Asked for the General Manager's office. Stayed nearly half an hour. With Russell Quinn.'

Alex lay flat on her face close to the stream in the garden of Shrimp Cottage. Hot sunshine after the rain had released the heady scent of lavender and honeysuckle, and played on her bare back and arms and legs. A lawn-mower spluttered in the distance, a motor-boat buzzed like a blue-bottle across the bay, children shouted on the beach and she could hear waves sucking hungrily at the pebbled shore. Safe and familiar noises.

She sensed a tickling on her back which a twitch of muscle failed to shift. She reached out a hand to scratch it, and encountered a long blade of grass; raised her head in irritation and turned, eyes coming slowly into focus.

Sitting on the grass beside her was Toby.

'Oh—it's you.'

'I saw you from the upstairs window. Or would you rather be left alone?'

'Yes, please.' She buried her face back in her arms.

Toby took a deep breath. 'Alex?'

'What do you want?'

'I want you.'

For a while she lay still and silent. Then her shoulders began to shake and she rolled over.

'Oh Toby, what an idiot you are! Here we are in the middle of death and disaster, and all you can do is make improper suggestions.'

'Well, it's not as though I've got much time left.' She stared at him blankly. 'I've got to go home in the morning, remember. So has Geoff. There hasn't been a lot of opportunity.'

Alex pushed herself up from the ground, brushed the hair back from her face and clasped her hands round her knees.

'Dear God, I didn't realize! There's been so much going on. I am sorry. It was really good of you to stick around so long. Is it really more than a week since you first phoned Melanie? It must be. This time last week,' she recalled wistfully, 'what was I doing? I was calling in at Susanne's to ask Melanie if she'd like Angela to spend the night here after we brought her back from *A Midsummer Night's Dream*. And being cross with her because she'd arranged that ghastly drinks session in your honour.'

Toby chewed on the blade of grass.

'And did you? Bring Angela back here?'

'No. Her mother didn't seem to fancy the idea much. Probably thought I wouldn't air the sheets properly.'

'Angela doesn't seem to get a lot of fun out of life for a girl that age, does she? Apart from horses.'

'Oh, I don't know. She's quite self-sufficient, is Angela. Reads a lot. The studious type. The fun will begin when she starts taking an interest in boys. Can't you just see Melanie putting them through their paces? Russell too, I should think. Look, Toby, I'm really sorry you're both leaving tomorrow. I shall miss you.'

'You will?'

'Of course I will. You must come back again some time, when—' she hesitated— 'when we don't have millions of tourists gaping at us everywhere we go: standing outside the house, trying to stare through the windows. I hardly dare go outside any more.'

'Thanks.'

'Oh Toby.' She reached out to touch his arm. 'I do wish things had been different. You'll never know how much I wish that—so that you could have seen us all as we really are. Not acting our heads off all the time, and being eaten up with fear inside.' Toby reached for her hand, but she snatched it away. Became suddenly brisk. 'I shall have to see Geoff before he goes. Where is he?'

'Gone to Susanne's to have a haircut. Says it's in preparation for going back to the office on Monday, but if I'm any judge he's after an invitation from one of them to invite him to stay over until Sunday. To give him an extra day down here.'

'To be in at the kill, you mean,' she said bitterly. 'What makes him think it will all be over by Sunday? Does he know something we don't?'

Toby sighed. 'I'm wasting my time, aren't I? You haven't any intention of accepting that you've got some pretty good friends who really care about you, and would do anything in the world to help you through a simply terrible time? All right, I know there isn't a thing we can actually do, but we are around, and we do care about you. And that includes me. One day you might remember that.'

He got to his feet. He had been a fool to take Geoffrey's advice. 'And since it's my last night —'

Alex let out a little cry. 'Don't say that, for God's sake don't say things like that.' She tried to smile. 'I'm sorry, I'm becoming a screaming neurotic. But you've no idea how sinister it sounded.'

'Sorry.'

'Well, go on. What were you going to say?'

Toby took a deep breath; smiled at her.

'Just an idea I had. That we might pretend none of this ever happened, and go out together and have some fun. Take the boat out, go swimming, talk about the old days, have a few drinks. Just you and me.'

She looked up, uncertain.

'But everybody will be staring at us.'

'Sod everybody.'

'What about Chris, and Geoff?'

'Sod them too.'

The left-hand dimple showed for a second; a glint of mischief sparked in her eyes.

'You know something—I'd love to.'

He reached out his hands to help her to her feet; put his arms round her and kissed her firmly. When he let her go there were crinkles of surprise between her brows.

'That was nice,' he said. 'Let's do it again.'

A few minutes later he replaced his glasses.

'Alex. There's something I want to say to you.'

Her blue eyes were still hazed; he must be careful, make allowances. Alexis Quinn was still in a state of considerable shock.

'Bless you, Toby. I always was rather fond of you, you know, and you've been a wonderful friend—'

He dropped her hands abruptly and grasped her by the shoulders.

'I don't want to be your wonderful friend, Alex. And I don't want to be a flaming brother to you either. You've already got plenty of those, if you ask me.'

Now he had gone too far. Much too far; much too fast. Alex was simply staring back at him in stunned bewilderment. From the beach came the sound of a radio broadcasting a cricket commentary. He kept his grip on her shoulders. Then she crumpled against him with a great shuddering gasp; snuggled her head against his shoulder, curled her arms around his neck and began to cry.

As the last customer left Susanne's at seven, she collapsed into one of the comfortable seats beneath the dryers.

'It was good of you to stay, Geoffrey. Helped take the pressure off quite a bit. You too, Melanie. You've been a tower of strength all week. I'd never have been able to cope without you.'

Geoff grinned. 'It's been a fascinating experience, sitting here eavesdropping; only shoving my diplomatic oar in when it seemed expedient. I don't know how you can bear all that tedious chat when you're trying to work. It would drive me mad.'

'It's quite fun, actually, most of the time. You learn a lot of very interesting things. Everything from hysterectomies to how to deal with errant husbands. That's right, isn't it, Melanie? The men who were here tonight aren't nearly so interesting. Melanie,' she exclaimed in exasperation, 'for God's sake put that broom away. It's after seven!'

The older woman looked up from sweeping a spotless floor.

'Thought I'd stay on a bit and clear up. We won't have Tracey coming in in the morning to do it, and it's Russell's turn on late duty tonight. We shan't be eating till later.'

'You'll do nothing of the kind. I'll do it tomorrow. You get along home to Angela. She'll be wearing out her welcome at the stables if you keep on using the Armstrongs as babysitters.'

Melanie looked belligerent. 'It's only been a couple of days,' she said coldly.

'Susanne's right,' said Geoff. 'You get off home and prepare me a boudoir—lavender-scented sheets and a jar of biscuits by the bed.' He put an arm round her shoulder. 'You've no idea how much I'm looking forward to some gracious living and a decent meal for a change.'

Melanie forced her arms into a green cardigan.

'We are always glad to see you, Geoff. You must ask young Toby if he'd like to stay on too. Unless he's got other plans, of course.'

Geoff smiled. If Toby had any other plans, he would soon ensure that he changed them. 'Great—I'll tell him.'

'You can tell him now,' remarked Susanne as she opened the door on to the road. 'We've got two lost children looking singularly damp but happy right here on the door-step. Why didn't you come in, you fools?'

Alex and Toby shambled in, scattering sand at every step.

'We thought you'd never ask,' said Alex. 'We've been out in the cold there for ages. Didn't want to intrude on any private conversations.'

It was almost like old times, thought Susanne: a free and easy congregation of friends gathered in the shop, relaxed and brown and looking as though their only thought was to enjoy the summer sunshine. Alex with blue jeans pulled up over her bikini, Toby in swimming trunks with a towel draped round his shoulders. Her spirits began to soar dangerously close to euphoria.

'We had a great idea,' Alex was saying. 'Since it's Toby's last—since Toby goes home tomorrow, we thought we'd ask you all to come and have a drink with us tonight— at the Green Dragon. And sod what anyone thinks, as Toby so neatly expresses it. No, Melanie, I wouldn't dream of saying that myself. I was far too well brought up. How about it, everyone? A sort of farewell party?'

Susanne raised her eyebrows at Geoff, who nodded.

'I've got an even better idea,' she said. 'Why don't you three come home for a meal with Stan and me first? Then we can all meet in the pub around—what—eight-thirty? That will give Russell time to get home and have a meal before we start.'

Melanie began to protest, but was waved down.

'You can bring Angela with you. It's quite legal so long as we stay in the gardens. We wouldn't dream of leaving her out. Off you go, Melanie, and feed your family. Stack the dishes in the sink just for once. It's not as though it does any good for us all to sit around being miserable.'

The euphoria lasted while Susanne waited at Shrimp Cottage for the others to change their clothes, and all the way up the path to Goldenacre.

It vanished abruptly as they emerged from the rhododendron bank at the top and came out into the open. Sitting on the lawn in deep conversation with Stan was Adrian Sheppard.

Susanne swallowed and licked her lips. Geoff let out a muttered expletive. Alex's grasp on Toby's hand tightened.

Jezebel was the first to spot their arrival, bounding over towards them slobbering with goodwill.

Adrian stood up. Smiled. Came over to meet them.

'Hello, Sis. Nice to see you again. Or don't you want me to meet your respectable new friends?'

Eight o'clock. For the last time Russell read through the final paragraph of his report with critical attention. The document was detailed but concise, a clear exposition of every issue which might be of significance. He folded it in two, reached for a large envelope. Addressed it.

The accountants could come now any time they liked; his letter suggesting a convenient day for them to visit next week lay, ready signed, in the out-tray. It had been a tiring day. Nor was he finished yet. There was one more appointment still to keep.

He dropped the empty whisky bottle into a bin of stainless steel; tipped two laden ashtrays after it. Glanced round the office, a pocket of light in a darkening building. Early in the morning the cleaners would be round, and another day would begin in the life of Cranston's Department Store.

He pulled the door towards him and left the room. Switched on the corridor light and locked the door behind him. Walked along to the stairway and down to the ground floor, its counters shrouded against the night. The spongy carpeting beneath his feet gave way to the hard echoing concrete of the passageway through stores and offices to the staff exit. He raised the emergency bar and let himself out into the loading bay, now empty and shadowed in the warm evening air.

He crossed the bay to his garage and opened the door; reached into his pocket for a bunch of keys, and unlocked the car.

There were scandalized villagers among the throng of visitors in the Green Dragon that night who could scarcely believe their eyes. Out in the pub garden, gathered round two of the rustic tables, were most of the principals in the events which had plunged Treskellan into a nightmare of suspicion and fear. Christopher and Alex Quinn with their niece Angela; Susanne and Stanley Hyson; and their two friends from the holiday let — Geoffrey Taverner and Toby Wilde. All apparently on the best of terms enjoying a convivial drink together.

Even more amazing was the presence among them of the youth from the caravan site whom the police had questioned at length three times in connection with the killings. Somebody ought to inform them.

Before very long, somebody did.

Only two familiar faces were missing — all credit to them. Russell and Melanie Quinn. What the shocked locals did not know was that Angela had brought with her a message of apology. Her father had phoned home from work to say that he would be detained in Port Laverock for a while, and would not be home till late.

Her mother was very disappointed and hoped nobody would mind if she just took a couple of aspirins and had an early night instead. And if Alex and Chris would take Angela back to Shrimp Cottage for the night, she could go to sleep with a clear conscience knowing that the girl was safely in their charge.

It was Chris who observed with a wry smile that this must be the first time in her life that Melanie had allowed an analgesic drug to pass her lips without protest.

Even Melanie, it seemed, was not invincible.

CHAPTER 10. SATURDAY

'Now that,' remarked Alex with approval, 'is what I really like to see. Two strong men engaged in polishing saucepans and hoovering the floor. I've never seen such a mess!'

Geoff pushed the cleaner towards her.

'If you had a really nice nature you wouldn't just stand there sneering. You'd give us a hand. We slept in. I always said this sort of thing was woman's work — nest-building and all that.'

'Just for that,' she retorted, 'I'll help Toby with the washing up.' She made a detour round the cases in the middle of the floor. 'My God, what have you been having for breakfast?'

'A bit of everything we had left over,' said Toby, dropping a light kiss on the tip of her nose. 'Seemed the best way of clearing out the fridge. We fed the really disgusting bits to the seagulls. Have a tea-towel.'

'What's all the panic for, anyhow?'

' "Tenants," ' quoted Geoff, ' "are requested to vacate the premises by ten-thirty on the day of departure, and oblige." We're engaged in obliging.'

'Ten-thirty! You're cutting it a bit fine, aren't you? Anyhow, you can't leave till Chris brings your car down from the village park, and he only went off with Angela ten minutes ago.' She looked despairingly at the clutter of possessions piled on the table. 'I hope you realize that you won't be able to live in chaos like this at Melanie's?'

'Good old Melanie,' said Geoff. 'Anyone who has two-tone bell chimes and blue water in their loo can't be all bad. If you'd been a real friend, you'd have let us move in with you next door.'

'With Chris as well? I've only got two bedrooms!'

'So? Just think of the fun we could have had.'

'And just think of what the neighbours would have said,' began Alex, only to break off unhappily. 'As if they don't have enough to talk about already. We were getting some very funny looks last night. Oh good, here's Chris.'

Geoff's car drew up on the double yellow line outside the window and Chris climbed out. Toby thought that he — like Alex — was looking better than he had all week. It could be, he reflected wryly, that there was something revitalizing in the act of speeding departing guests.

'What, no coffee?' demanded Chris.

'You're joking,' retorted Geoff. 'We've only just cleared up the last lot, and I'm not going to get done for illegal parking just to satisfy your insatiable lust for coffee.'

Chris sighed; picked up one of the cases.

'It's quite legal to do a quick park for the purpose of loading up. I'll get this lot into the boot and you can buy me a drink lunch-time instead. Melanie's going to have a fit when she sees it all.'

'Not a bit of it! Anyway, only half of it's mine. Young Toby here is still having trouble with his finer feelings. He's a nice lad, Alex. I should hang on to him if I were you. He thinks it dreadful that we should impose on Melanie and dirty her sheets just for one night.'

'She won't mind,' said Chris. 'Melanie adores having company, and it will do her good to have something else to think about. Hello, here's Angela come back to help. Ask her, if you don't believe me.'

Geoff was on the floor, kneeling on his suitcase as the girl came in out of the sunshine.

'Come to watch the circus, Angela? Good girl, we need all the help we can get. Be an angel and empty that repulsive binette into the dustbin out the back, will you?'

No one answered.

He looked up in surprise. Angela stood like a sleep-walker, her eyes enormous. Very slowly he got to his feet, glanced at the others. Toby was twisting a tea-cloth in a ferocious grip as Chris dropped the case; went over to her.

'Angela, love, what's up?'

She shook her head helplessly.

'I don't know how to tell you. It's Daddy. He's dead.'

There was a thump as Geoff sat down heavily on the arm of the couch. The colour in Alex's cheeks drained away, leaving her features etched with shock. Chris put both arms round the child and held her close, his face like granite.

'The police were up at the house. They've been there for ages. They say he killed himself. And wrote a letter saying that it was him — he killed them both: Tracey and Caroline.' She looked up at Chris with terror in her eyes. 'It's not true, is it?'

'Of course it's not true,' said Alex sharply. 'It couldn't possibly be true.'

Toby struggled against the conviction that he was living through a nightmare of appalling proportions. He looked at Geoff. The man was sitting on the couch arm, shaking his head from side to side in stunned disbelief.

'*Russell?*' he whispered. 'Not *Russell!*'

Someone had to say something, do something. Toby knew he must be the only one not stupefied beyond reality; heard his own voice, impotent with good intention, saying he'd make some coffee.

But as he spoke, the frozen scene disintegrated into farce with the arrival of a buxom lady, overalled and indignant.

'You lot ought to be out of here by now, you know. Half past ten, that's the arrangement. Got another five places to get cleaned before I finish, and I've had to come all the way from Port Laverock. So I'd be obliged if you would kindly all get out of here and let me get on with my work.'

Detective-Inspector Bracken laid down the final page of

Russell Quinn's signed confession, and closed his eyes.

'All nicely buttoned up, you think?' asked Golspie.

'You've got to say this for the man, he was methodical to the end. Chapter and verse, times and motives. It all seems to fit. Amazing that a man about to take his own life could express himself so—so dispassionately.'

'He'd had a good deal to drink before he got round to it. Still, you do wonder how he must have felt going out alone to that garage and closing the door behind him, jamming a length of hosepipe over the exhaust and leading the other end into the car. Then switching on the engine and just sitting there, waiting.'

'Yes, must have taken a lot of courage. Or fear.' Bracken sighed. As Golspie had suggested, it was a nice tidy ending. Ridiculous to feel so cheated.

'There won't be any trial, then?'

'That's the way it looks.'

'How about his wife? I know she's in no fit state to say much yet, but surely she suspected something?'

'It's possible. I'd think most of the people concerned must have started suspecting one another during the week. At the same time, Russell Quinn was quite a dominating man in his own way, and she struck me as being a remarkably devoted wife. Almost submissive. It could be that it simply never entered her head that he might be the killer.'

'If only she'd realized he was missing earlier than she did.'

'Yes. Natural enough, though, for her to have gone to bed early. She must have had one hell of a week, one way and another. To wake up in the morning and find he was not in bed beside her must have been an appalling experience. At the same time—' Bracken picked up Russell's handwritten statement— 'there are one or two things I'm not happy about. The Tracey Harman killing for one—he gives precious little detail, though that doesn't necessarily mean it's not true. And his claim that he drove Caroline's car back to London. Not that it wouldn't be physically possible to do all he says he did that night, but he was taking a hell of a chance. And Melanie Quinn must certainly have known he was away from home all night, but she never mentioned it when we questioned her before.'

'What does he say about it?'

'Not a lot.' Bracken consulted the confession. 'Says he told his wife he was going back to the office to work late, and would spend the night there, something he did from time to time when things were busy at Cranston's. According to the assistant manager, that's true enough.'

'Then why didn't Mrs Quinn say so when we questioned her the first time? She swore they were both at home.'

'Frightened, perhaps, that we might suspect Russell then? People do that sort of thing from the best of motives sometimes. Caroline Quinn was his sister-in-law.'

Sergeant Golspie stroked his chin. 'And the girl — Angela — couldn't help?'

'No. She'd had three late nights on the trot playing Titania in the school play. Her mother let her sleep well past breakfast-time, long after Russell was back from London. It's interesting that Russell says he went on believing he could get away with it on the principle that if there was no evidence and no confession, he'd be quite safe.'

'He was right at that,' nodded the sergeant.

Bracken smiled grimly. 'Don't you believe it. We'd have got him in the end. And I still fancy the idea that there was an accomplice. Someone who really drove the car back to Paddington. It's time we had another go at Adrian Sheppard. Nothing will persuade me that young man was only down here for the good of his health.'

Melanie closed the bedroom windows. Although the sun

still shone outside, her hands and feet were frozen. She shivered, and bent to open one of the deep drawers at the base of the white fitted unit built against the wall. Found a heavy cardigan in thick Aran wool she'd completed only last month.

This one was in rather a nice shade of mustard yellow with brown wooden toggles. She had thought the style might be a bit young for her, but Russell thought it was lovely. So she'd made it. It would go quite well with her fawn Crimplene skirt. That was the beauty of fawn, you could wear almost anything with it. Except navy, of course; or black.

She reached her hands behind her head to struggle with the silver catch at the back of the pearls Russell had given her as an engagement present. She always had trouble with that catch; it got snagged up in the wool of her cardigans. If he'd been here, he would have fastened it for her.

She must not think about Russell. Not now. Her private agony of grief must wait for expression until she was alone. There would be no public display of emotion.

Melanie held her face close to the mirror. The skin didn't look at all healthy, but that was only to be expected. No one would expect too much of her today. Not today.

Her brown suede handbag lay on the bed: the big double bed with the white quilted headboard and great fat duvet covered with orange geometrical shapes angled against the brown. Like the curtains. Really nice. She blinked rapidly and reached for a tissue. It might be better, perhaps, to replace the bed with a single divan one day. Less empty and lonely and cold.

Just at that moment, Melanie would have given anything to have thrown herself across her marriage bed and given way to a great desolation of weeping.

But she must not let Russell down. Whatever he had

done, it had been done for her and Angela, and for the best. She must cling to that knowledge, and ensure that his terrible sacrifice had not been made for nothing. Prove herself worthy of so great a love.

She dabbed at her smarting eyes. Began to breathe in deeply, rhythmically. All those years stretching out into a future she would have to face alone. It would not be long before Angela would go away to make a life of her own, and she would be left behind. Even a life sentence was not all that long these days: eight, nine, ten years? He would still have been young enough for them to have had many years together. The rest of her life was going to be an eternally long time.

On her own. Russell had always taken care of everything. Even the house would now be hers, after only four monthly payments off the mortgage. Funny how she could think of something like that now — quite shocking, really. She wasn't sure how she'd be fixed financially apart from that, but not to worry. Russell would have taken care of all that.

Angela put her head round the door, hesitated, and came into the bedroom. She looked oddly adult, protective; their natural roles reversed: the child eaten up with concern for her mother.

'I thought I'd come down with you, when you're ready.'

'That was kind of you, dear.'

It was almost like having a son, taking on the responsibilities of his father. Someone to be leant on, relied on, prepared to take over from Russell in the way he had taken over from his father, in looking after Chris and Alex. Russell would have liked a son. Melanie felt the piercing pain of remorse and guilt for all those things left undone in their life together.

Angela put her hand out nervously, let it hover close to her mother's shoulder and then withdrew it, embarrassed. Stood quietly to one side, hands clasped together. She

really looked very nice in a plain navy dress with a re-
peating motif of small white aeroplanes: the darkest
clothing she possessed. Very suitable. She was wearing
tights as well, and the navy shoes she wore to church.

'Mummy?'

'Yes, dear?'

'Are you quite sure you want to go through with this?'

'Quite sure, darling. The family has a right to know.'

Angela's hands began to twist: 'The family, yes. But I
don't see what it's got to do with anyone else. They've all
come over from Goldenacre. Geoff and Toby and the
Hysons. They've even brought Adrian.'

'That's right, dear. I invited them.' She took her
daughter's hand, surprised to find it as cold as her own.
'It is what your father would have wanted.'

'I don't see how you can say that.'

'You must trust me, Angela, to know exactly what your
father would have wanted.'

'You know what,' muttered Geoff, 'this is getting more
like the state opening of parliament every minute. All we
need now is a fanfare of trumpets. Do we all stand up
when she comes in?'

'How should I know?' said Toby testily. 'Do you have to
make remarks like that?'

'Yes, it stops me from screaming. Any minute now the
french doors will fly open and Hercule Poirot will leap
into the room—'

He stopped in mid-sentence at an imploring glance
from Susanne, her hand clutched in Stan's, her brother
beside them on the couch. On the far side of the room
Chris sat hunched in one of the big armchairs with Alex
perched on the arm beside him, talking quietly. The
facing chair stood empty, an island of uncut moquette
afloat on a sea of polished parquet squares.

There was, Toby felt, an impressive dignity about

Melanie when, haggard and pale, she appeared in the doorway, the victim of more unhappiness than anyone could possibly imagine. She crossed the room and sat upright on the edge of her seat while Angela, chin held high, sprawled with studied grace at her feet. She looked up at her mother with a shy smile of encouragement.

'Thank you for coming,' said Melanie. 'I only want to do what Russell would have wanted. That I should tell you why he had to do it. So that you could try to understand.'

'Are you saying,' asked Alex in a strangled voice, 'that you knew? You knew all the time?'

'Of course not, dear. At least not until we had reason to believe that you, Adrian, had been arrested. It was then he told me. Because he would never have let you take the blame for something you hadn't done. Russell was not that sort of man.'

Geoff nudged Toby. 'For God's sake, we can't let this charade go on. Heaven only knows what she'll be saying next. The poor woman's half out of her mind.'

Susanne frowned. 'Are you telling us that you knew — knew all about everything on Thursday, and you were still able to come to work as usual on Friday?'

Melanie's left hand twisted at a wooden toggle on her jacket.

'Look,' said Geoff desperately, 'why don't we all shut up and let Melanie say what she wants to say without us shoving our oars in all the time.'

From behind half-closed lids Toby was watching Alex, sitting impassively beside her brother. Then Melanie planted her feet more firmly on the floor, and he found his eyes following the tracery of small blue veins on her bare white legs. She crushed her right hand round a handkerchief before speaking, almost as though she had been rehearsing the words all day.

'When we bought this house, we'd been expecting

rather more money from the sale of·Goldenacre than we actually got, what with expenses and sharing it with Chris and Alex. That was when things first began to go wrong. On top of that, there were rumours that Cranston's was to be sold up later in the year. Russell had a lot of financial worry because we'd taken on an awful lot of extra commitments.'

'You knew about all this, did you?' asked Adrian unexpectedly.

'Oh no, of course I didn't. Russell would never have wanted to worry me with things like that. But he was determined to protect me and Angela.' She opened out the handkerchief and inspected it. 'So he tried his hand at speculation, I think it's called.'

'Where I come from they call it gambling and embezzlement,' remarked Adrian. Susanne glared at him, and Melanie flushed.

Who was it, thought Toby, had said that Russell had always been something of a gambler? Was murder the ultimate form of gambling? And where did Caroline and Tracey fit into the picture?'

'To begin with, it seems he did very well, very well indeed. Then things began to go wrong. And the firm's accounts were going to be audited quite soon.'

Stan Hyson sighed. 'Why on earth didn't he come to me?'

'There was no need, you see. It wasn't a tremendous amount, really, which was involved at the time. And when Adrian turned up out of the blue one day looking for a cottage to rent beside the sea, it seemed quite providential. With Pendrufford standing empty.' Alex gasped, opened her mouth and was silenced by Chris. Melanie looked reprovingly at Adrian. 'And if you had only told us the truth about that, none of this would ever have happened.'

Adrian bent forward. 'Now I know you're upset, lady,

but don't you start trying to make me feel guilty. I've had enough of being hassled because of you. The police have been on my back all afternoon suggesting I'd been an accessory. All I did was make a perfectly straightforward business deal with your husband.'

'I don't know about it being straightforward. You told us a story about a prominent politician wanting a secluded retreat for a quiet weekend with a lady who was not his wife.'

'Well, what if I did? He was keen enough to have the money. And I offered to pay him well; very well indeed for one lousy weekend.'

He sat back, injured, and Melanie passed the palm of her hand wearily across her brow.

'Please,' she pleaded, 'I'm doing my best. Russell wrote a full confession for the police. But I am quite sure your name would not be mentioned in it. Russell has always been a very considerate man.'

Across Toby's mind flitted an image of Geoff's snapshot of Caroline Quinn, and he felt physically sick.

'Unfortunately, he went over to Pendrufford after work that Friday to make sure the tenants had everything they wanted. There was no answer, so he let himself in — we always keep a spare key in the shed — just to see that everything was in order.'

'Did he now?' said Adrian grimly.

'And you, Adrian, will know what he found. The room stacked with crates and boxes full of silver and antiques. When he heard footsteps coming towards the house, he just panicked. Hid behind the door and jumped on the intruder; he was simply furious that he had been used, incriminated in such a way.' She studied the sandals on her feet. 'By the time he realized his terrible mistake, it was too late. Caroline was dead. I am so sorry, Chris, so terribly sorry.'

There was a long silence.

'I am afraid he behaved very badly after that, but he was so shocked and horrified that he simply didn't know what he was doing. He came home for the car and took Caroline to—to where she was found.'

Toby wondered how Russell must have felt during the rescue of Jezebel, and shivered.

'He'd taken Angela's bicycle in the estate car, drove to Port Laverock and left the car at Cranston's. Cycled back here, then drove Caroline's car up to London, catching the train back from Paddington.' She fought back her tears. 'I suppose you might say he was very lucky, really, that nobody saw him. He was very careful, of course.'

'It looks to me as though he was trying to throw suspicion on to Chris,' said Alex shortly.

'Oh no, dear. Russell would never have dreamt of doing that. You must remember he was in a dreadful state of shock. He was only trying to divert suspicion from down here. No one else knew that Caroline was at Pendrufford.'

'And you still say say you knew nothing at all while this was going on? Oh, come off it, Melanie!'

'Alex, I swear to you that I didn't. He told me that he was going back to work late at the office and might stay on overnight if he didn't finish till late. He's done it before. Of course, I didn't like to tell the police that. I'm afraid I did persuade Russell not to mention it, in case they started jumping to the wrong conclusions. There didn't seem to be any need.'

Angela shifted slightly.

'Then there was Tracey.' Melanie's hands began to tremble. 'And the phone call to Chris. Tracey said something in the shop the day Chris arrived about the post office van, and Malcolm being late on his round. In quite a nasty sort of way. And when I thought about it, I wondered if she'd been the one who'd sent the call, who knew about Caroline's car being down here.'

'And you mentioned this to Russell?' asked Adrian.

'Yes, of course. We were all wondering who'd made that call. Then—' she looked round at them all unhappily— 'it seems Tracey called in at Cranston's that afternoon looking for a record. Russell met her on the shop floor and offered her a lift home. And somewhere close to the coastal path—'

'And then spent the rest of the evening playing tennis with us?' whispered Susanne.

'Well, he had to, didn't he, dear? And then when Toby told him how if the police had no evidence and no confession, people often got away with breaking the law, he felt that he might be safe after all.'

'So why did he change his mind?' asked Adrian gently.

Melanie's expression softened.

'Because he was a very good man. He couldn't live any longer with the knowledge of what he had done. It was the only honourable thing that he could possibly do.'

'Stan was right about Russell,' said Susanne as she poured drinks back at Goldenacre. 'He always said Russell was far more likely to fall apart under strain than Melanie.'

'That woman amazes me,' said Adrian. 'Imagine having the guts to play the truth game like that on the very day her husband killed himself.'

'Well, she's almost senseless with shock, of course, but it was quite in character. She loved him only just this side of idolatry, and was clearly determined to preserve his memory as a loving, caring man of integrity and honour among those who were his friends. Totally bizarre, of course, but very brave.'

'Talking of the truth game,' remarked Adrian, 'I didn't let you down, did I, Sis? I was a credit to you, don't you think? Family loyalty at its very best. Just suppose I'd let slip that my sister was married to one of the most successful villains in the business?'

Susanne handed him a drink.

'I hope you realize what you've put us through. Stan finished with all that a long time ago, and don't you ever forget it. To go to the Quinns after we'd refused to get involved was a rotten trick.'

'But Pendrufford was ideal! We were able to land the stuff and ship it out with no trouble at all.'

'Maybe. But you can imagine how we felt, with all the trouble at Pendrufford, and then Tracey. It was the happiest day of my life when Caroline's car was found in London. I was sure then that your shady friends had nothing to do with her disappearance. Tell me, Adrian, did you actually meet Melanie, or was your business only with Russell?'

'Yes—I met both of them.'

'So that accounts for how she knew you were well-spoken. I was quite suspicious of her at one time.'

'It seems you were suspicious of me as well,' he retorted.

'No, Adrian. I was worried sick, but I'd never believe that you had killed anyone. How much did you make out of that consignment of goodies you cached away at Pendrufford?'

'That would be telling. Very successful operation, that. Picked up my share in a pub at Torquay the night young Tracey died, poor kid. Made alibis quite a problem. I did consider asking you to give me one, but I did think better of it. I gave Russell Quinn his cut yesterday morning, poor devil. I hope it helped him to cook the firm's books.'

'And are you going to get away with it?'

'I reckon so. I don't think the law was on to us at all, but it was a close thing. We shipped the stuff out on its way to the States late on Friday night. If we'd known there'd been a murder done in the house that day, we might have lost interest in the whole exercise.'

'Funny thing, causality,' remarked Susanne as Stan came in with the dog. 'If Jezebel hadn't gone wandering off on her own, Caroline would probably never have been found. And if old Dr Quinn hadn't died, we would never have bought Goldenacre and Adrian would never have come here looking for a safe house; and Russell would never have died. Tracey and Caroline would still be alive today.'

'You can go a lot further back than that,' said Stan, pouring himself a drink. 'If your father hadn't died in prison, God rest his soul, I'd never have sought out his children and arranged for your upbringing. And Susanne would probably have married someone else when she grew up. And that—' he kissed her— 'would have been quite terrible.'

'You two were a great partnership,' said Adrian with pride. 'Dad always said you were the real brains of the organization. You must have felt nearly as bad as we did when he was sent down.'

'Yes,' said Stan softly. 'That was the end of everything. We'd worked together ever since National Service days. But I was really just a sleeping partner when it came to the action. All I did was the research and a bit of legwork. Your dad was the professional, the real expert. He was a great man, your father, and a loyal friend.' There was a small silence before he spoke again: 'What do you think we ought to do about Melanie? Leave her over there all by herself?'

Susanne shrugged. 'It's so difficult, but yes, I think so. She does have Angela. It's Chris who's got nobody. He's lost his wife and his brother. All he's got left is Alex.'

There was a sudden flurry of movement from the big couch which stood facing the window. Susanne's hand flew to her mouth.

'My God! The lodgers! I forgot all about them! How long have you two been sitting there?'

Toby and Geoff poked their heads round the corners of the couch.

'Actually,' said Geoff, 'we've both been fast asleep, right up to the point where Alex's name was mentioned. Then I thought you might say something which Toby should not be allowed to hear, so we decided to wake up.'

Toby more shamefaced, began to stammer:

'Look, Susanne, we really didn't know what to do. We thought you realized we were here to begin with, and by the time you were deep in family reminiscences it seemed a bit late in the day to break the news. So we decided to have a nap.'

'That's right,' agreed Geoff. 'Out like a light, both of us. We never heard a word.'

The neat leather travelling clock on Angela's bedside table ticked away fussily, dominating all the other sounds of the night. Three hours ago she had come to bed after the visitors had gone home, her mother warmly inviting them all to return to The Shrubberies whenever they might wish. Russell, she had said, would have wanted that.

Angela lay back on her pillows, eyes open wide, and wondered if she would ever see some of them again. Toby? Adrian? Geoffrey Taverner too might feel that Treskellan held more than enough memories for him ever to feel he wanted to return. Even Chris and Alex — how would they ever be able to understand when she, who loved him so much, was so bewildered?

Her mother had tried to persuade her, as she had tried to persuade herself, that — misguided and terrible as his actions had been — they had been committed out of his overwhelming wish to protect and care for his family. Dearest Mummy, going off alone to the master bedroom, looking so desperately ill and weary, still with time to fuss over her child with such loving concern, such desperation. Angela had prayed to God to look after her and comfort her; to care for Daddy too.

Beside the busy little clock lay the white sleeping pill,

evil with temptation. So easy, so cowardly a way to escape the thoughts spinning, whirling, rushing at her out of the dark. Thoughts about the night Toby arrived for drinks, and Chris had phoned from London, worried about Caroline; and on his first night in the village it was he, with Alex, who had found Tracey's body at Pendrufford Point. Then Angela herself on the way back to the stables, finding Jezebel out unattended, and calling to her. The mineshaft rescue, when she had been so happy and relieved that the dog was safe. If she had never called the dog, Caroline's body would never have been found, and Daddy would still be alive. It was, in a particularly horrible way, all her fault. Angela's eyes flooded with tears, scalding, bitter.

At least he'd had a chance to be proud of her school report, her performance in the school play. It all seemed so long ago. Yet, while she was on stage that last night, they said he was killing Caroline. Even though it had been a terrible mistake. Alex was a bit uptight because she'd said she'd have Angela to stay with her for the night, but her mother hadn't fancied the idea. So they'd dropped her off at home instead. Quite late. The hall and landing lights were left on, but her parents had gone to bed. So she'd thought. Now it seemed it was just her mother who'd gone to bed, tired after an evening cooking for Toby's party next day.

Don't think about it any more.

Angela had found it hard to sleep that night too, after so much heady applause and excitement. A different sort of wakefulness, pleasant and enjoyable. But if she went to sleep now, she knew she would have to wake up again. That was terrifying.

She made a bargain with herself: she'd go to the bathroom first, and if she were still awake in half an hour, she'd take the sleeping pill. She reached out a hand and switched on the bedside light, screwing up her eyes as the room sprang alight: a pretty room, papered in a tiny floral pink and white print, fitted with carpeting of deep rose pink. She slipped out of bed and tiptoed over to the door, opening it with care; crept out on to the landing.

As she stood outside the bathroom in her pyjamas, there came a sudden recollection of the last time she had gone to the bathroom in the middle of the night. That Friday, when she couldn't sleep either, after the play.

But she hadn't gone in, because someone was already there. She had heard that tickling cough which was so familiar that she'd barely noticed it at all; she had simply known that her father was there before her. And she'd gone back to her own room until she heard the cistern flush, and listened to the soft footfalls heading for the main bedroom.

The door had been opened, then closed.

In the middle of the night.

CHAPTER 11. SUNDAY

Alex jumped down from the Pendrufford jetty and sat in the stern of her dinghy.

'Right. We can go now.'

Chris cast off and began to row quickly away from the shore, heading north across the bay past the village with strong, easy strokes. As they passed well clear of the harbour, she sighed.

'I suppose this is cowardly and reprehensible, but I cannot take another minute of being a brave little woman without losing my sanity altogether. I'm so confused I'm almost past caring any more. Almost callous.'

'Yes, I know,' said Chris quietly. 'There's no need to feel guilty about it. After all, none of us is superhuman.'

'But *Russell!*' She stared up at the little church on the

hill. 'If we had any decency at all we'd be getting ready to support Melanie in the family pew.'

'Melanie won't be going to church this morning. She's taken more than anyone could be expected to stand already. But Alex,' he said gently, 'we've talked most of the night. You must be still for a while — that was why we came.'

'Yes. Susanne said she'd keep an eye on The Shrubberies and would call over at the first sign of movement. She was scared stiff, of course, but insisted she'd cope till we got back.'

'You saw the boys off all right?'

'They set out bright and early. They're going in convoy as far as the motorway intersection north of Bristol; Toby leading the way in case he breaks down.'

'Nice lad, Toby.'

She looked across at him and tried to smile.

'And you can spare me unsubtle remarks like that, Chris dear.' She leant over the stern and trailed her hand in the water. 'He did invite me,' she said at length, 'to go and stay with his family one day, when all the inquests and funerals and general furore are over. Well, he didn't put it like that, but that's what he meant.'

'Very proper of him. I approve.'

'Did you like him?' she asked curiously.

'I didn't see much of him. He seemed a nice lad. Not that I'd ever be the best judge of any man who wanted to marry you. I'd be bound to be prejudiced against him, up to a point.'

Ahead, a few small woolly clouds were scampering across the blue of the sky. A gull screamed and swooped low past the bows.

'I never thought,' said Alex, 'that you might feel that way as well. I thought it was just me.'

Chris smiled and shook his head at her.

'I do think, though, that you should do something

about getting a job after the summer.'

'Perhaps,' she admitted without enthusiasm. 'Will you go back to your job, to the joys of James Barncroft Comprehensive?'

He looked surprised at the question. 'Of course.' Her face fell. 'I'll have to go back to the flat before that, of course, and do some sorting out.'

Her eyes lit up. 'I'll come with you, and help.'

Chris rested on his oars; watched the village disappear from sight behind the cliffs.

'No you won't,' he said gently. 'Thanks, Alex, but this is one thing I'd rather do on my own. There are so many memories that belong only to the two of us—Caroline and me.'

'Yes, I can see that.' She stirred restlessly. 'I suppose it is time I did something useful with my life.'

'I tell you what. I'll give you a lift as far as Surrey and drop you off there so that you can spend some time with Toby. How about that?'

Alex tried to laugh. 'If you insist, I might just do that.' She watched her brother for a while. 'Chris, there are three questions I'd like to ask, and then I promise I'll stop.'

'Ask away. I'll try to answer them, if I can.'

'The night Caroline died, you said you got a phone call in the middle of the night. Do you think that it was Russell, checking from Paddington that you were at home? After all, he must have wondered why Caroline was at Pendrufford.'

'I'd like to think it wasn't, but it could have been.'

'The other two are tougher. What were you really doing that night, and why on earth did Caroline come down here?'

Chris sighed. 'I really did go for a drive to the Chilterns, but was unwise enough to take a very upset girl—a pupil of mine—with me. But why Caroline should come here—'

he shrugged— 'your guess is as good as mine. We did
have a disagreement and she was upset about something,
but I don't know what. I can only imagine she drove down
here on impulse, and didn't get a chance to phone and
tell me. But that's something, Alex, I'm never going to
know.'

In a pretty Devon village Toby flagged Geoff down and
pulled into the forecourt of a cottage smothered in
rambler roses; pointed to the wooden board offering
morning coffee.

'Car's beginning to overheat,' he called. 'Fancy some
tea and toast?'

They went inside, stooping low beneath the doorway;
found themselves alone in a low beamed room with fresh-
cut flowers on dark polished tables. Geoff sat comfortably
with his back to the wall and pondered the menu.

'I never was much good at early morning breakfasts,'
said Toby with a nervous laugh.

Geoff eyed him shrewdly. 'Don't try to kid me, my lad.
You just couldn't bear to go off home without a final poke
around in that unsavoury can of worms we left behind.'

Toby flinched. 'Well, there wasn't much chance to talk
at Goldenacre. What with none of them turning out to be
what I'd always thought. Well, Adrian did, perhaps; but
Stan was a bit of a surprise. Susanne too.'

'They do say the West Country's full of retired villains.
And old Dr Quinn must, as the other saying goes, be spinning merrily in his grave. What should really happen is
for Chris to marry Melanie and restart the whole dynasty.
Then you could pick up the pieces left over once Alex sur-
faces again.'

Toby's anger was deflected by the arrival of a cheerful
girl to take the order. When she had disappeared through
the beaded curtain:

'Do you have to be so flippant about it all? It seems

quite wrong to me that Adrian should get away with his little enterprise.'

'Well, it would, wouldn't it? But he was only following the advice you were giving Russell—admit nothing and you'll get away with anything so long as there's no evidence. I'm sure he and Melanie spent a long time pondering those words of yours. Everyone is innocent until proved guilty beyond reasonable doubt, that's what you said. You can't have it both ways. I suppose you'd have Stan clapped in irons too, to stop him living comfortably off the proceeds of the crimes he planned and Jason Sheppard carried out all those years ago?'

'It seems to make a complete mockery of the law to me.'

Geoffrey gave a coarse laugh. 'Spare me your high moral principles, Toby. There must be dozens—hundreds—of villains who are amusing and delightful people. Even Russell, one of the nicest men I've ever known, had his sticky little fingers in the till at Cranston's. If Adrian Sheppard had never set eyes on Pendrufford—'

The girl arrived back bearing a laden tray. Toby helped her unload it on to the table and thanked her. Shoved the toast-rack towards Geoff and began to pour the tea.

'You were saying that if only Adrian hadn't chosen Pendrufford,' he prompted, looking up.

Geoff sliced savagely at the butter.

'Oh, for God's sake, can't you give the whole bloody thing a rest? I'm sick of talking about it, sick of thinking about it. If only this hadn't happened, if only that hadn't happened—if you go on thinking along those lines you come to realize that we're all in some way responsible for three dreadful deaths. And two of them were my closest friends.'

Toby was smitten with remorse. In all the drama of the past week, he had nearly forgotten that. Geoff Taverner

could not have many friends. His future must seem very
bleak.

'I'm sorry, Geoff,' he said quietly. 'Really sorry.'

He began to butter a slice of toast, glancing covertly
across the table at his companion, sitting with clenched
hands, face furrowed with pain. At last he exploded into
anger.

'If you really want to know, if it hadn't been for me,
none of them would have died at all. It was because of me
that Caroline came to Treskellan. I'm the missing link.
Shall I tell you why?'

'No—for God's sake don't! It's none of my business. I
don't want to hear about it.'

'Then you're damn well going to. You remember those
snaps of Caroline I showed you? Those were only two
shots taken from that film. There were others. One night
last summer we all went for a moonlight picnic—Caroline
and Chris, Russell and Melanie and me. We'd taken some
bottles of wine with us and were slightly the worse for
wear when we decided to go in swimming. All good clean
fun.'

He stirred the spoon round in a dish of marmalade.

'The next bit sounds a bit unsavoury. When we were
getting dressed I took some photographs. A couple of
them were of Caroline. *Au naturel*, at least from the waist
up. She looked terrific. That beautiful body, sprinkled in
droplets of water, and the moonlight on the sea behind
her. When she'd sobered up a bit, she became terribly
embarrassed and ashamed about it, so I told her that it
had been a duff film; that none of the shots had come
out.'

'But they had?'

'Oh yes. They were fantastic. Quite beautiful. Out of
this world.' He refilled his cup. 'Just before I came away
on holiday I wrote to them both—we always kept in
touch, on and off—saying that if Caroline couldn't tear

herself away from Chris for one lousy weekend while I was at Treskellan it would be the end of our wonderful friendship and I'd just have to post them some amazing snapshots I'd taken last summer. Dear God!' He gestured wildly. 'I only meant it as a joke, though it sounds a pretty sick one now.'

Toby looked up at him.

'But she could never have thought you were serious! And even if she had, surely Chris isn't that much of a Puritan?'

'Not Chris, no. But Caroline was. Convent-educated, lapsed Catholic; she had this terrible thing about sin. And as no one seems to have a clue why she came down here, not even Chris, I can only imagine she thought I was planning a particularly nasty kind of moral blackmail.'

'Blackmail! Now you're being ridiculous.'

'I only wish I were.'

Toby was frowning. 'But why on earth should she think that? What were you supposed to be getting out of it?' His eyes met Geoffrey's, and he looked away. 'Oh God—I see what you mean. Lonely gentleman meets gorgeous girl— I'm beginning to get your drift.'

'You're a nice lad, Toby, with a very nice mind. That makes you just a bit slow to catch on, at times.' Geoff twisted his stocky fingers together. 'What—what distresses me most is the thought that Caroline probably died believing I could do such a thing to her. But I've thought about it a lot, and I feel sure she came down to Treskellan to sort me out.' He smiled. 'She would have done too, if any of it had been true. But she got herself killed instead.'

'Geoff, you can't possibly blame yourself. Unless you feel you have to, of course.'

'If that's a polite way of saying I've become paranoid, then you're probably right. I felt sick that night at Russell's when I heard she was missing, and that Chris was being questioned by the police. Why do you think I asked you to move in with me? I wanted to know exactly what was going on, what people were saying and thinking. Alex would find out from Chris, and with any luck, she would confide in you. I wanted to know if he had ever seen that letter of mine, or if Caroline had kept it hidden. And when her handbag was found to be missing from her car, I didn't know what to think. I was using you, Toby.'

'Fair enough. I'd probably have done the same myself.'

'That's charitable, at least. Stan and Adrian are not the only ones who've been concealing something unsavoury. Susanne knew all about Adrian and Pendrufford, not to mention Stan's ill-gotten wealth. Melanie was making a fat profit from doing a spot of quiet subletting of Caroline's cottage to get Russell out of debt, and I still think Chris was giving a highly edited version of what had gone on at the London end. The only person who emerged from the whole thing with any credit at all, it seems to me, was Russell.'

'*Russell?*' Toby gasped. 'Oh, I see what you mean. Doing the honourable thing and all that?'

'Exactly. You must never forget that, young Toby.'

'But — Good Lord! — the man was a double killer!'

'Oh yes. Didn't make a bad job of that confession at all; though the version Melanie gave us was decidedly thin in places, as I'm sure you noticed. A bit short on exact times and locations. In the circumstances one could hardly ask for greater clarification. I wonder if she realized that.'

'Was it because of her that he killed himself, do you think?'

'Of course.'

'But — even if he'd been found out — he must have known that wives are normally protected from being charged as accessories after the fact, however much tongues may wag.'

'Melanie wasn't an accessory. Melanie was the killer.'

Toby's cup clattered on to its saucer.

'That's a dreadful thing to say!' He stared at Geoff. 'Are you sure?' he added more quietly.

'I could never prove it in a court of law, if that's what you mean. In my own mind, I am absolutely certain. Shall I tell you why, so that you can go back home leaving no stone unturned?'

Toby thought of that careworn, kindly lady, and nodded miserably.

'Right from the start I was determined to find out what had happened to Caroline, and after Tracey died, I felt sure that Caroline was dead too. Killed either by Chris or one of the rest of us. If only I could piece together what everybody had said or done or thought, or even suspected, it might be possible to assemble a sort of jigsaw puzzle. You thought it was extremely bad form, didn't you?'

Toby nodded. 'I did then. You should have told me — I'd have tried to help.'

'No, I couldn't do that. For a while I thought Alex and Chris might have been in it together. Alex was the only one who lived alone and had no job to tie her down. She could have been implicated quite easily. Stan, too, worried me. He didn't have a job either, and could roam around quite freely. But the first time I knew that Melanie had to be involved was the morning after Caroline's body was taken from the mineshaft, and the whole place alive with rumours about a sex maniac on the loose. She'd actually left Angela alone in the house and come to work, knowing the child would have to walk a mile through lanes and tracks to the stables. The way Melanie fusses over that child — well, it was crazy. When Susanne mentioned it she began to react in the character of a worried mother, but not till then. Susanne phoned Stan to tell him to get over to The Shrubberies fast, but I still wasn't happy about the Hysons, so I got up there too. It was later that it dawned on me that the only explanation was that Melanie knew Angela was perfectly safe, and that meant the killer must be either herself or Russell.'

'That was on the Thursday morning? The day it rained?'

'Yes. So I started backtracking over everything that had happened from the time of Melanie's party in your honour, when Chris first phoned with the news that Caroline was missing. I remembered Angela saying how tired her mother looked, and she did, too. Hardly surprising after what she'd been up to the night before. And the way she'd been so startled when she thought Alex said you were a detective; that must have given her a nasty turn for a moment. And it was Angela who said they ought to phone Pendrufford to see if Caroline was there. Neither she nor Russell had thought of it, almost as though they knew it would be a useless exercise, subconsciously at least. But she wouldn't let Alex go with them, remember? She probably wanted a chance of a private word with Russell.'

'So Russell was implicated, right from the start?'

'I don't think there's any doubt about that. He didn't have a lot of choice, poor devil, torn between conflicting loyalties as he must have been. Then there was the police inspection of Pendrufford for evidence, and they found it virtually clean of any prints at all. It was Melanie who said she'd springcleaned it ready for Chris and Caroline. My guess is that she did clean it out for Adrian and his gang, but went back later to remove, not just their prints, but any of her own she might have left.

'The next indications were from the night we played tennis at Goldenacre. Melanie is a very powerful player; quite strong enough to overpower a slip of a girl like Tracey; even Caroline, if she were tired after a long journey and was jumped on unexpectedly. After all, she'd hardly expect to be attacked by someone she knew so well, would she? And there were one or two other things. She spoke about Adrian in an unguarded moment as though she'd met him personally, and Russell managed to throw a violent coughing fit to stop her in time. And of course she was on hand when Russell asked you about the chances of a random murderer being caught.'

'Objection,' interposed Toby. 'I accept all that you say, but why pick on Melanie? It seems to me much more likely it really was Russell.'

'Why? Because he was a man? No. What pointed more towards Melanie was the suspicions they voiced aloud. At least Russell was decent enough to put his money on some nebulous random killer who lurked in the Bournemouth environs; but Melanie didn't hesitate to suggest Chris might be involved, in a subtle sort of way. All that talk about they'd probably had some little disagreement. I shouldn't think Russell let her carry on in that vein for long, so she switched to some secret lover that Caroline had tucked away somewhere. And when it all got too close to Treskellan, she switched again, to Adrian.'

'Mm, but it's hardly evidence.'

'I never said I had any hard evidence. One last point, and you can order some more tea. Last night Melanie said she'd guessed from some remark of Tracey's that she'd been the one who'd seen Caroline's Fiat on Friday night. I couldn't ask her, so I checked with Susanne. Her recollection is a bit hazy, but she thinks it was not so much what Tracey said, as the manner in which she said it, sort of suggestive and insinuating. Something about having mistaken the post office van for another vehicle. Now both the van and Caroline's car were small and red. But it seems to me that it's a very tenuous connection for anyone to pick up, unless they had a small red car seen in the village that night very much on their minds.'

'So Tracey had to die,' said Toby thoughtfully, 'because Melanie thought she might be dangerous. But she said as much. Said she'd told Russell about it. The loyal wife, come hell or high altitude.'

Geoff leant forward eagerly. Stopped to call the girl

and ask for more tea. Turned back to Toby, his eyes
alight.

'Oh, do use your brains. Think about them for a second as the people they actually are—their personalities!
Let's suppose, just for argument, that it was Russell. He
kills an intruder in some sort of panic, and then discovers
it is Caroline. Christopher's wife. Russell has spent most
of his life in absolute devotion to Alex and Christopher.
The closest of brothers, those two. Always have been. If
he had killed her—which I beg leave to doubt—he'd have
been absolutely appalled, shattered beyond belief. This is
a man who can't cope with terrible happenings—look
how he took his own life! Do you really believe he calmly
dumped her body down a mineshaft and drove her car
back to London in a manner that would be bound to in-
criminate Chris?'

'So what actually happened?'

'I would suggest that Russell never went near Pendrufford
that night. Why on earth should he? But Melanie now,
she always did like to know what was going on in the village. I can easily believe that she went snooping on some
pretext to catch a glimpse of the alleged famous politician
on his dirty weekend, and found the place full of nicked
antiques. Very nasty, that, with the image of the highly
respectable Quinn family at stake. Probably meant to get
the hell out of the place with the utmost despatch. Then
in walks Caroline. To find her own home requisitioned
and Melanie standing over a roomful of stolen loot. Caroline would have hit the roof and wouldn't have come
down till the police were in possession.'

'So, according to you, it was Melanie who panicked?'

'Yes. Probably for the first time in her life. Her family
was threatened by Caroline, and so she had to be silenced.
It's my guess the panic reaction didn't last long; just long
enough. After that—well—we all know how good she is at
organizing things.'

'Go on,' said Toby grimly. He looked up to find the waitress at his side with a fresh pot of tea. When she had gone he filled their cups as Geoffrey went on speaking.

'What Russell was reported to have said about what happened next is remarkably complicated—all that cycling around and so on. I think it was much simpler than that. I think Melanie, back under control, walked back home, fetched the car and took Caroline's body up to that fenced mineshaft. The safest place in the world. I sometimes wonder how many other bodies lie at the foot of some of those shafts, their killers never detected. But there was the car to be got rid of—Caroline's car. It could have been dumped there too, but that would be more tricky. So she went home to Russell and told him what had happened.'

'Just like that?'

'I don't see what else she could do. She needed an accomplice. And at least he was in the clear. Give Melanie her due, she doesn't lack courage, and would never have involved him if she could have helped it. She left directions with him, and drove the Fiat to London, ditching it close to Paddington Station so that she could catch the overnight train back to Plymouth.'

'Plymouth?'

'That's what I would have done. Of course, being a woman, she'd realized the significance of the handbag still in the car—no woman travels far without her bag—so she got rid of it somewhere. Meanwhile she'd told Russell to leave the lights on for Angela and go to bed before she got back, so that the child wouldn't wonder where her mother was. I bet she wished she'd accepted Alex's offer to have Angela for the night after all. Russell spent the night trying to come to terms with his own private nightmare, and left the house at the crack of dawn to pick Melanie up from Plymouth and get her back home as quickly as possible.'

'So he didn't spend the night in the office?'

'Of course he didn't. That was probably some botched-up story they'd concocted against the chance that someone had been up and seen the car get back. They could say he was coming home from the office for breakfast. But there was no need to use it, then. Angela slept on late, and there were few people in residence this time last week on Mafia Mews. If Russell's nerve had held out, they would probably have got away with it. But his nerve broke, and he must have resurrected the original story to protect Melanie from suspicion.'

'And Tracey?'

'Ah!' Geoff scratched his head. 'That's my weak link, the only piece of the jigsaw that's still adrift. Somehow Melanie knew she'd be on the coastal path that afternoon, or early evening. I don't know how, but neither can I accept that Russell gave her a lift home, persuaded her to get out of his car, led her down on to the path, and then choked her and sent her hurtling to her death. Didn't Tracey object at all? Did she just walk like a lamb to the slaughter? Not young Tracey! I think she was jumped on by someone hiding in the bushes. And my instincts persuade me that it must have been Melanie. Not a shred of evidence to support it, though.'

'And that,' asked Toby, 'is the case for the prosecution?'

'That's it. She must have told Russell about Tracey too, which only added to his torment. If he hadn't cracked, no one need ever have known. But after a week of hell, he opts for a quiet spot of *felo de se*. Don't blame him, poor lad. Eight days on the rack would be enough for most of us. And before he goes, he sits down and writes what he hopes will be accepted as a full confession. No more enquiries, no sensational trial, and Melanie is in the clear.'

'If you are right,' said Toby slowly, 'and only if you are right, do you think she should be allowed to stay free after committing two horrible murders and driving her husband to suicide?'

'You mean she should be punished according to the law, I take it?' Geoff smiled knowingly: an evil smile. Toby recoiled, and then remembered how Geoff had loved both Russell and Caroline, by his own admission his closest friends. 'Rest assured, young Toby, that Melanie — if she is guilty — will be punished for all eternity in a way the law would never allow. Her adored Russell offered up on her behalf as a human sacrifice? After she had killed two people on his account? Everything Melanie ever strove for was done for Russell, and, in the end he let her down. He left her on her own. All that remorse and guilt, the terrible loneliness, and above all the certain knowledge that as long as she lives she can never gain relief by confiding in a living soul. You see, Toby, Melanie's punishment is going to be entirely self-created. She really is what everybody says — a very good woman.'

There was a long silence; then Geoff looked across.

'Is that not punishment enough?'

'It's too terrible to think about.' Toby shivered. 'And where does Angela fit into this — this appalling scenario?'

Geoffrey sighed deeply. 'Poor child. The fruit of Russell's loins, the living embodiment of their union. God help her. Melanie is going to cling to her for the rest of her life. Still, I suppose it's better than that she should ever know the truth.'

They paid the bill, wandered out into the sunshine of the forecourt.

'I don't think I'd better risk the motorway,' said Toby, 'with the car in this state.' He held out his hand, smitten with shyness. Geoffrey shook it warmly; climbed into his own car.

'Geoff? Will you want to go back again,' asked Toby on impulse, 'believing what you do?'

Geoff's face crumpled again into that attractive grin

he'd come to know so well.

'You're all confused, aren't you? Never mind, lad, I could be wrong.' He fastened his safety-belt and started the engine. 'So long, young Toby. Have a safe journey.'

There was a discreet disturbance as the organist came into the church from the vestry, sheet music in one hand. Very soon he would start to play the voluntary, and the ringing of the church bell would stop.

Melanie sank to her knees, head bent low, eyes closed behind black-gloved hands.

'Almighty and most merciful Father, we have erred and strayed from thy ways like lost sheep, we have followed too much the devices and desires of our own hearts, we have offended against thy holy laws . . .'

The house was still and empty, windows open, curtains closed. Angela roamed from room to room, touching, fondling, stroking as she went. All the familiar things, fabrics, laminates, wood, door handles.

Now the church bell had stopped, and God had not answered her prayer for help. She could still remember her father coughing in the night. She could still remember, too, how she'd seen Tracey in Port Laverock as she waited for the school bus. Tracey wouldn't join the queue; said she wanted to walk home by the coastal path, and Angela had mentioned it to her mother over tea, before she went off to the stables.

She walked through to the lounge, where two big arm-chairs flanked the hearth, the couch pushed back against the wall, all three reflected in the parquet flooring.

She went back to the hall; looked at the telephone on its mahogany stand: one of the latest models in turquoise green, its flex curling round and round and round.

She picked up the receiver and began to dial: nine—nine—nine.